BLUES BONES

BOOK ONE

RICK STARKEY

Cover by Nina Gautier Gee and Rick Starkey
Interior Layout by KellyHashway.com

First Make It Magic Edition 2019
ISBN: 978-1-7331425-3-3 (paperback) / ISBN 978-1-7331425-4-0 (e-book)
First Leap Edition 2016 ISBN: 978-1-61603-072-8

To my wife, Betty Starkey
(AKA Twinkles at Make It Magic),
for telling me I had so many books about writing that I
should become a writer.
And letting me!

and

In memory of Hubert Starkey, my dad,
for being the first to tell me a scary story when
I was a kid. His retelling of the thing looking for its big toe
always had a new and surprising ending that made me jump
each time he said, "Gotcha!"

chapter ONE

I COULDN'T MOVE. EXCEPT FOR MY FINGERS, which were trembling so bad I couldn't stop them. The whole school was staring at me.

"And now, here is Rodney Becker," a voice announced over the P.A. system.

The entire gym went quiet. The spotlight blinded me, my palms sweated like a hot snowball, and the butterflies in my stomach turned into a school of raw fish. Finally, my one chance to show the world, or at least Mountain Side Middle School, that I was the next bona fide blues guitar superstar.

After fifteen seconds of silence, I turned and yanked the guitar cord from the amplifier. Someone turned the thermostat to high heat, and my face burst into flames. At least that's what it felt like. I actually got a standing ovation with thunderous applause while I raced to the gymnasium door.

"Rodney!" Max's voice reverberated through the empty hallway along with his footsteps as he ran up to my side. "What just happened?" I knew from his smirk he was holding back a laugh.

"Nothing," I said.

"Yeah, I know. But why?" He skipped a couple times like a little kid then matched my gait step for step. I felt like we were synchronized robots.

"I couldn't move. It's like rigor mortis set in or something."

"When they said your name, you looked cool with all those blue lights behind you. But when the spotlight came on, you looked like an idiot."

I stopped walking. "I didn't see you standing up there in front of the whole world. You think it's so easy?"

"I didn't mean it like that." He turned. "I just—"

"Forget it." I sprinted to catch up with him.

I gave Eddie Manford's locker a kick as we walked by. "I didn't hear my backing track. Was it even playing?"

"Yeah, your karaoke track started and was still playing when you bolted off stage. Too bad you didn't go on before Eddie. He nailed every note. He's great."

"Thanks a lot."

"But you're better. When you play," he added.

Max followed me to my locker. "Maybe you're right. Maybe I wouldn't have been so nervous if I'd played first." I pulled my guitar case from the locker then shoved the fiesta red Stratocaster and cord inside. "I don't know how I'm going to beat him in the Music Today Theater's talent show if I can't play in front of people."

Eddy Manford is the sorriest, stupidest, lamest, greatest guitar-playing idiot on the planet. He's not afraid to play in front of people. It's like he's in his own special world. On *and* off stage.

The bell rang, and the halls filled with a mob of kids. I imagined they were my fans chasing me, until I heard some of the things they said. Stuff like, "Hey, Rodney, they give guitar lessons down at the Guitar Outlet." And, "Hey look. It's the Blues Fool." The name stuck and turned into a chant on the way to the buses.

For the first time since second grade, I sat in the front seat behind the driver. If I didn't walk down the aisle, no one would notice me. That plan didn't work.

"Maybe he should play air guitar," someone on the left side said.

"No wonder he plays the blues," came from the right.

"Yeah, when he plays," the blond girl sitting beside me added without looking up from her book. She looked like she might be in third grade. How did she know what had happened?

In the mirror above the driver, I watched the guys in back high-fiving each other. Just seven point six miles and it would all be over. I would be home.

When I got off the bus, I turned and took a bow to the ones shouting at me from the windows. I figured idiot fans were better than no fans at all, so I blew them a kiss, shook my guitar case above my head, then turned and trudged the dusty tenth of a mile from the bus stop to my house.

Mom stopped vacuuming when I walked in. "How did it go?"

"Don't ask." I ran to my room.

I counted her footsteps as she walked down the hall. Ten, eleven, and then, *knock, knock, knock*. She must have taken giant steps because it usually took at least fifteen when she walked normally.

"Rodney, open up."

I opened the door and dove onto my bed. She propped herself up with her shoulder against the doorframe and pulled off the *CSI*-looking rubber gloves she used when she cleaned. "So, what happened?"

"Nothing, Mom. That's just it. I couldn't play." I rolled over and faced the wall.

"What do you mean you couldn't play? You play all the time."

"I froze up and couldn't move. Like when I tried to play in church that night. I couldn't play a note."

"Well, I'm sure you'll do better next time."

I rolled back over and sat up. "That's what you said the *last* time. Today *was* the next time. I'm cursed."

I prepared to hear her story, for the thousandth time, about her famous eighth grade speech. When her turn came, she threw up on the podium. Any time someone talked about stage fright, she told that story.

She walked over, gave me a hug, and left without the story. It was kind of depressing that I didn't merit a retelling of it.

"I'll never make it," I said out loud. The Music Today Theater's guitar contest was one month away. How would I win a competition when I couldn't play a note in my own school talent show? Guess I didn't have to worry about how to spend the two thousand dollar prize money or about ever getting a recording deal. How many recording companies would give one to a thirteen-year-old anyway?

I sat staring at a poster on my wall of an auditorium filled with people attending a rock concert. The photo was taken from behind a guitar player at center stage. How could anyone perform with so many people watching? Ten thousand strangers. Twenty thousand eyes, give or take a few considering some might be blind or blind in one eye. I had looked at the poster maybe a million times, pretending I was on stage with them. I even knew where the prettiest girls were. Guess I was too busy picking them out because for the first time, I noticed a rabbit's foot hanging on the back of the guitar player's strap. How could I have missed that? It's weird how something can be right in front of your eyes and you never see it.

I'd heard of a superstitious ballplayer wearing the same lucky underwear, without washing them, to every game. Some martial arts guy even drank his own urine before his competitions. I never thought about a musician needing a lucky rabbit's foot. It made me wish for a good luck charm or some kind of magic spell to help me get over my stage fright.

I fell asleep playing my guitar again. Playing without an amp, with my eyes closed in the dark, was very relaxing. It was great practice, too, learning to hit all the notes without looking.

Saturday morning, I woke up holding my guitar. I called Max to see if we were meeting at the Guitar Outlet before we hit the arcade at The Track. We were, so I rode my bike down Ridge Road to Teaster Lane. The traffic wasn't too bad for a Saturday, but it took a full ten minutes to go the two miles to the Guitar Outlet. The city of Pigeon Forge, Tennessee wasn't big, but there were always a lot of tourists driving around. When I rode up, Max's bike was lying on the sidewalk.

"Hi, Rodney. How's it going?" Lenny asked when I walked in. Lenny was cool for a store owner.

He would let me play any of the guitars. Even the expensive ones.

"Pretty good. I need strings, and I want to check out those digital recorders on sale, even though I can't afford one."

"There's the man to talk to about recording." Lenny pointed to a tall man standing at the checkout counter. "Mr. Cory Williams. He's in the process of adding a new mixer to the recording studio in his home."

We walked to where Cory was flipping through an owner's manual. *Allen & Heath GS-R24M Recording Console* was written across the top.

"Hey, Lenny," Cory said. "How you strung today?"

Cory and Lenny laughed and shook hands.

"Somewhere around a low E," Lenny said, and then he looked at me. "Cory, I'd like you to meet Rodney Becker. He's an up-and-coming guitar player. I told him you're the one to talk to about the recording equipment."

"Hello, Mr. Rodney Becker." Cory offered his giant hand.

"Great to meet you, Mr. Williams," I said as we shook. His fingers felt like they were as long as a guitar neck. He looked familiar, but I couldn't place him. His gray hair against his black skin made him look distinguished, not old, even though he had some wrinkles. He reminded me of a movie star, but I couldn't remember his name.

"So, you're getting ready to record?" he asked.

"No, I'm just dreaming about the recorders. One day I would like to record some songs."

"Well, as soon as I get my studio put back together I'll be booking recording time a couple days a week. I might even need a volunteer to record while I work out all the bugs." He smiled and looked at Lenny.

"He can play your style," Lenny said. "Rodney's the one you heard playing last Saturday when you were here. He's one of the best young blues players around. He'd be great in a studio, but he's kind of shy when people are watching."

My face heated up.

Riiiiing! The deafening squeal of feedback filled the shop. Lenny and I turned at the same time and shouted, "Max!" Max was a wannabe soundman. He loved anything electronic, especially if it had to do with sound, like amplifiers and P.A. systems.

"Sorry," Max called from the other room. "Just trying to ring it out." That was always his excuse since he had read an article about how to ring out a

P.A. system by finding the frequencies where feedback starts and then cutting those levels.

"You're ringing *us* out," Lenny shouted.

"I'll get my strings and get him out of here," I said. "I need a set of Boomers. Oh-nines."

Cory handed me one of his business cards. "Here you go, Rodney. Give me a call on Monday, and we'll set up a time for you to come over. It'll give me a chance to try out the new mixer, and you might even get a CD out of it."

"Wow! You serious?"

"Yeah." He nodded toward Max. "You can even bring your friend, Feedback, if you make him promise not to touch the amps."

"I promise. Thanks," I said. "See you all."

"Keep your strings tight," Lenny said.

I walked toward the door while reading Cory's card. It was so fancy I could feel the letters when I rubbed my fingers across them. *Wow*, I thought, *I may have just landed my first recording deal.*

Riiiing!

"Max!" all three of us shouted.

chapter TWO

MONDAY MORNING, PEOPLE ACTED ALL WEIRD IN the hall.

"How's it going, Becker?" Billy Johnson asked. Billy Johnson had never spoken to me before in my life.

Wade Bennit shouted, "Rock on!"

After they passed, I could hear them laughing. I had hoped everyone would have forgotten about my talent show performance, or lack of, but just about everyone I passed made a comment.

When I walked into Mr. Brannon's science class, Eddie Manford was at my desk. "I made you a star," he said and smiled one of his weird, contorted smiles. He looked like he had gotten a Botox shot on the left side of his mouth and in his left eyebrow.

"What's that supposed to mean?" I asked.

"You'll see."

Kyle Reed, Eddie's sidekick, laughed and tried to high-five Eddie. Kyle looked like a weirdo when Eddie didn't high-five him back. Kyle smacked the air and quickly stuck his hand into his jeans pocket.

The tardy bell rang, and everyone scrambled to be seated. Mr. Brannon turned to the board, erased a giant number seven, and replaced it with a giant number four. The lines now said, "You've had six weeks. Now you have four days to complete your science project." When he finished, he tapped the marker three times on the board and said, "I will accept no excuses." He loved countdowns so much that he always had one going.

I wondered what grade I would get if I dissected Eddie's brain. Probably a zero because there wouldn't be anything to dissect. Eddie used to be okay until his father invented some new electronic device so airplanes could transmit their flight data to a satellite or something. No more looking for black boxes and stuff if a plane crashed. His big quote was, "Duh, with all the cell phone and communication technology, why didn't the rocket scientists think of it?"

Since then, Eddie could get anything he

wanted. We used to play together until one day in the sixth grade I wouldn't let him see Mom's digital camera I'd sneaked out and took to school. I'd told him it was too expensive for him to even touch. He hadn't had much to do with me again until his family got rich. After that, he made sure I knew about all the new toys he got. Especially his cell phone. He was always showing Max and me videos he had recorded on it then asking if we had any cool ones to share. "Oh," he would say, "I forgot. Cell phones are too expensive for you two."

After school, I found out what Eddie had meant when he said he made me a star. I had received a strange email.

From: *anon2too@gmail.com*

Subject: *Unplugged music video: An Eddie Manford Production*

Message: *Hey, check out this video. It has already received 1,384 hits.*

Rock On!

I clicked on the link titled "Unplugged." By the time I got to the video, the count was up to 1,854.

The video started with some cool blue lights

and a guitar player's silhouette in front of a deep blue background. Then the spotlight hit him.

It was me. I looked cool. For a few seconds anyway. No wonder everyone at school had acted funny when I walked by.

I called Max. "Hey, you get a weird email?"

"No. Why?"

"Hold on," I said. "I'm going to send something to you." I clicked forward.

"Isn't it wild how you can send something all the way up to a satellite in space and within a few seconds it sends it down to my computer?"

"You get it or not?"

"Yeah, I got it," Max said. "Who is Anon-two-too? Sounds like a ballerina."

"It's got to be Eddie. It says it's an Eddie Manford production, and he told me he made me a star."

"I don't think this makes you a star. It makes you look like more of an idiot than you are. I mean, than you were."

"You're not helping," I said.

"Impressive," Max said. I heard him laughing. "It's pretty sweet that when you turn and unplug your guitar the screen returns to the blue lights and starts over."

"Yeah, he may win an Oscar or something for best worst video recorded on a cell phone."

"Hey, did you call that Cory guy yet?" Max asked.

"No, do you think he was for real?"

"Only one way to find out."

I opened the top drawer of my desk and picked up Cory's business card. "Hold on a second." I typed in Cory's web address. "Wow, this guy *is* somebody."

"What do you mean?" Max asked.

"I just went to his website. He's a songwriter for some television shows. Says he's with a company called Big Entertainment. You know the show *Safety Rulz*?"

"Yeah, why?"

"That's him. He wrote the songs for it."

"Wow, you might be a star after all. Call him. Then call me back."

"I might," I said then clicked on a link to Big Entertainment.

"Rodney? You still there?"

"Yeah." I was busy reading and had stopped talking. "I'll let you know." I ended the phone call without telling him bye.

Cory was amazing. He had written hundreds of

songs for Big Entertainment and had even won some awards.

No bones about it, Cory Williams is a perfect fit for Big Entertainment...

Cory Williams has been with Big Entertainment for twelve wonderful years. He writes and records over ninety-five percent of the music used on our top three shows...

Cory Williams wins Parents' Choice Award for Children's Song of the Year...

Cory Williams signs up for another year with Big Entertainment...

The list went on.

I picked up his card to dial. My fingers trembled the way they had at the talent show. I took a deep breath and pressed the last number.

chapter
THREE

I THOUGHT FRIDAY WOULD NEVER ARRIVE. I WAS using Mr. Brannon's countdown, but not for the science project. My countdown had one more day to go.

Mr. Brannon gave me a B and said I could have spent a little more time thinking of something more original. I had stretched a rubber band around a candy box covered in duct tape and explained how sound is produced on stringed instruments. Max hooked a bunch of lemons together with wires and some nails he took out of his gutter to make a battery that powered an MP3 player. It played a recording of me performing the new song I wrote. Sometimes I wondered if he and Eddie were brothers that had been separated at birth. Not that the two of them were anything alike, it's just that Max had a brain for electronics like Eddie's father.

I guess the week took so long because I was excited about going to Cory's on Saturday. Well, I was excited until I got home from school and saw Dad's green-and-rust F150 pickup in the driveway.

I walked in and rushed to my room. Mom followed. I could hear Dad going through the refrigerator like a scavenger. He'd make himself at home even though he hadn't lived here for five years. Mom said our house was his personal walk-in/dine-in mini storage because of all the things he left.

"I don't want to go with him. You know I have plans for tomorrow."

"I know you do, but if you don't go now, there's no telling when the next time will be."

"Tell him I'm sick or something. Tell him I've got a ton of homework. Or I have a report due." I sat on the bed, staring at my poster and wishing I were on stage somewhere playing loud rock music. Dad hated rock.

Tell him it's his turn to wait, I thought. *Tell him my music engagement is more important than he is this time. Oh, but I'll try to make it up to him the next time.*

Mom made me go talk to him.

"You guys on a diet or something?" Dad was still rummaging through the refrigerator. "What does she do with all that child support I send?"

"She gambles and drinks, and we starve," I said.

"Yeah, right. If she did stuff like that, we'd be able to get along. We might even still be together." He turned with a pack of bologna, some single cheese slices, and a jar of mayonnaise. "Want one?"

"No, we're out of bread. So, what's going on?"

"I just thought I'd stop by to see you for a few minutes before I leave." He put his plunder on the table and spread his hands apart as far as he could. He looked like a magician just finishing a trick with the "Ta-da! Look at me; I'm special" moment. "I'm heading to Music City, son. Rusty, from the band, got us a gig in this club in downtown Nashville. A lot of the music industry big wigs hang out there. This could be our big break."

"When are you leaving?"

"We're packing up tonight and heading out in the morning. I just wanted to come to see you before we go."

Come and brag is more like it, I thought.

He wrapped two slices of cheese in a slice of bologna, grabbed a can of Pepsi, and propped himself up against the sink.

"Oh," I said. "I thought you were coming to get me for the weekend like you said you would last time." I gave him one of Mom's "make you feel guilty" glares. Tight lips, squinted eyes, and all.

"Oh, God. I'm sorry. I forgot. That was two months ago. I can't remember stuff like I used to. How about after I get settled in out there, you come to Nashville for a weekend?"

"That would be great," I said. *That would be the worst weekend of my life*, I thought. I would be stuck in some little apartment while he was out playing and drinking all night. "But I thought we were doing something now."

"It's a date. I promise. As soon as I'm settled, I'll come get you so we can spend some time together. You can come out and hear some *real* music. Country!"

Great. Guy's night out at the Grand Ole Opry.

"Maybe you'll see country is where it's at." He picked up the Pepsi to take a drink then realized it wasn't open. "That's where the money is. You still playing that rock stuff?"

"Yeah, I like it. I'm going to be in a contest the Music Today Theater is having."

He rolled another two slices of cheese in a slice of bologna and took a bite.

"Well, don't play that junk you've been doing. Maybe I can teach you a few country licks and stuff. I'll email some new songs you can learn. If you want to win, you need to be playing country."

"Dad, just leave it alone." I grabbed the cheese wrappers off the table and threw them into the trash can. "I know how to play country. That's all you could ever teach me." I put the mayonnaise and the rest of the bologna back into the refrigerator. "I can also play blues, jazz, classical, and rock. I don't play for you anymore." My stomach churned again. "Besides," I shouted, "you're never around to hear anything I play."

His smile faded, and his gaze went to the floor.

"Jason," Mom said, storming into the kitchen, "when are you going to leave him alone about playing country music? We don't like it. Rock can't be all that bad. After all Dolly Parton, the queen of country herself, recorded *Stairway to Heaven*. Led Zeppelin is about as far from country as you can get. Their song was good enough for her."

"Shows how much you know." Dad stuffed more bologna roll into his mouth. "Kitty Wells is the queen of country music."

Since Mom came in to run interference, I ran to my room and slammed the door. I should have known he would have more important things to do than be with me.

I called Max because he could usually take my mind off things. "You still going to Cory's with me tomorrow?"

"Absolutely! It's going to be cool seeing a real recording studio."

"It's a home studio," I said. "It probably won't be like the ones we see on TV or in movies."

"Doesn't matter. It's a studio, ain't it? Maybe he'll let me help mix the sound."

"Look, you don't touch anything, and don't ask to touch anything, or you'll never go back. You're only going because he said you could come with me." I didn't bother to tell him that Mom said I couldn't go by myself. If he had known that, he would have tried to make some kind of deal with me.

"Okay, I promise. I won't touch anything. Unless he lets me."

Through the wall, I heard Mom and Dad arguing. I knew it wouldn't be long before he would be leaving. She always made him go when things got to that point.

"Well," Max continued, "I might learn something by watching him mix."

"Hey, Max, Mom's knocking. I gotta go. I'll see you tomorrow."

"Rodney, you doing okay in there?" Mom called from the hallway.

I pulled open the door. "Yeah, I'm fine." Even though I didn't want to go with Dad, I guess she knew I was bummed he hadn't come to pick me up. I was used to it, though. I had stopped getting my hopes up about two years ago. He'd done it too many times.

The best thing about Dad playing country music was that he'd given me an old Fender Stratocaster some guy had given him because he owed Dad money. Dad told me it was a rock guitar and country players should play a Telecaster or a Les Paul. The Fender was a lot better than my old Strat wannabe copy. The copy didn't even have a brand name on it. It played okay, but it wouldn't stay in tune. Especially when I used the whammy bar.

Before I went to bed, I checked the "Unplugged" count. It was at 3,352 hits.

Saturday finally came. Mom had to work a double

so she made me promise to finish my to-do list before going to Cory's. I hadn't thought about it, but I kind of had a problem. To get to Cory's I'd have to ride my bike. To get my guitar there, I'd have to carry it. For the first time, I wished I'd owned a gig bag instead of a hard shell case. I would never be able to carry the case while riding the bicycle. I thought about using the guitar strap and letting the guitar hang on my back. Bad idea. My strap was so worn that sometimes it would come off the strap button while I was playing. One good bump and it could be over. I had until 2:00 to come up with a solution.

The ride to Cory's was nice. I'd forgotten how cool Mount Le Conte looked in the distance. Dad used to promise that when I was old enough to hike up there, we'd stay at the lodge on top. He used to drive us to the park at least once a month in the summers. He'd always say how lucky we were to live so close to the Great Smoky Mountains National Park. It's probably why they named the place Mountain Side. I wondered how many tourists came to Pigeon Forge and Gatlinburg for the arcades, go-cart tracks, museums, theaters, and Dollywood but never made it to the national park.

Cory Williams lived a mile and three-tenths from our house. I must have looked like an idiot riding along with my old Transformers sleeping bag strapped to my back by a belt and a bungee cord. It would have kept me toasty warm if it had been freezing outside, but it felt like I'd sweated a gallon by the time I got there.

Cory's house looked like something out of one of those fancy house magazines. When I rode up, Max's bike was lying on the sidewalk next to the front door. I worried what he might be doing inside.

I parked my bike on the driveway next to the garage. The bungee was wrapped around me so tightly that when I unhooked it, the end slipped out of my hand and flung itself around me like a giant rubber band. The sleeping bag-covered guitar started to slide down my back, so I bent forward to slow its fall. Just as I caught it, the end of the bungee cord came around and slapped me in the jaw. That's when my reflexes sent both hands to the left side of my face. I guess I was lucky it didn't stick in me like a gigantic fishhook. For a moment, I couldn't move. I wasn't bleeding, but it felt like I'd been slashed open like someone in one of those horror movies. The guitar made a dull thud when it bounced on the cement driveway. I jerked the Strat out of the bag as if being quick about it would lessen the damage. It looked okay. At least the neck was still attached to the body.

From somewhere behind me, I heard the shrill laughter of a hyena.

"Impressive, Becker. You okay?"

It was Max. He'd been checking out the swimming pool. I was glad he hadn't gone inside the house yet.

"Yeah, I think." I rubbed my jaw. It was sore, but it didn't feel swollen. "I'll let you know later if it turns blue."

"This guy must be rich. You've got to check out the pool."

Max grabbed my shirtsleeve and pulled me toward the chain-link fence. "Maybe he'll let us go swimming sometime."

"We're not here to swim. It's not like we're his best buds or anything. Now come on. Pick up your bike and stand it on the driveway."

"Kickstand's busted."

"Well, at least move it out of the way."

He hopped on his bike, rode it to the driveway, and propped it up against mine.

I pressed the doorbell. After about thirty seconds, Cory's voice came from a small speaker to the right of the door. "I'll be right there, Rodney."

"Look, dude." Max pointed to a small camera mounted above the door. He closed his left eye and opened his right one as wide as he could. Tilting his head to the left, he got about three inches from my face and said, "He's got his eye on you."

"Yeah, and he's probably watching you be an idiot. Knock it off."

The door opened, and Cory waved us inside. "Welcome to my castle. I'm glad you could make it."

Castle was right. The place was like something out of a movie. Most of his furniture looked like expensive antiques.

"Would you two like something to drink?" Cory asked when we walked by a bar. Max and I looked at each other. His eyes opened wide. I knew mine had done the same, along with my mouth.

Cory laughed. "It's only soft drinks, juices, and flavored water. I call it the Minor's Club. I don't allow anything in the place a minor couldn't have."

"Do you have Pepsi?" I asked.

"Sure. And you, Max?"

"You got grape?"

"As long as you promise not to spill it on the carpet. Grape is the worst to get out."

"How about Sprite?" Max changed his mind. For once, he'd used common sense.

There were hundreds of photos on the walls in gold-trimmed black frames. Each had a caption telling who was in the picture. They said stuff like *Bones with Carlos Santana* or *Bones with Robin Trower*. He even had one that said *Bones with Eric Clapton*.

"Do you know all these people?" I asked.

"Yeah, our paths used to cross quite a bit. Some of us still get together every now and then."

"So, who is this Bones dude?" Max asked. "Never heard of him, but he's in all of these."

Cory stopped pouring the Sprite. He sat the can and glass on the counter, stood up straight, and then a puzzled look swept across his face. "Well, some say he was one of the world's greatest guitar players. Others think he's a fool for leaving the fame and torture of stardom to write songs for six-year-olds."

"That's crazy," Max said. "Who would do that?"

I elbowed Max in the ribs and whispered, "I think it's him, doofus."

Cory laughed and raised his right hand. "Guilty. I'm the fool."

"I meant it would be crazy to put up with all that torture," Max said.

"Sorry," I said. Leave it to Max to call a world famous guitar player crazy.

"No worries," Cory said. "Those days were a little before your time."

"Max, look at these." I walked over to a black and gold showcase. I wanted to change the subject because I felt bad that we had never heard of Cory even though he must have been famous at one time. Inside the case, there were some trophies along with a bunch of guitar picks on little stands. Each pick had an autographed note card telling whose it was along with a date.

"You collect guitar picks?" I asked.

"Yeah," Cory answered, "it's kind of a hobby of mine. The only ones that make it in there are from guitar players I've had the pleasure of playing with."

"Does Richard Starkey play guitar with drum sticks?" Max asked.

"Oh, I've done some work with Ringo. He signed his real name for me. He signed the other side of the card Ringo Starr."

"Wow, you know the Beatles?" I asked.

"I know Ringo. We've worked on some kid's stuff together. The picks up top are some of my personal favorites."

"Look." Max pointed to a row of three small display boxes sitting on top of the showcase. "Here's one that says Jimmy Page."

I knew who Jimmy Page and Stevie Ray Vaughan were, but I had no idea who the third one was. It said Blues Mullins.

After Cory finished pouring our drinks over ice in some fancy glasses, we followed him through a doorway beneath a sign that read: "Come on Down."

The lobby at the bottom of the stairs reminded me of a doctor's office with its four black leather padded chairs and sofa. The coffee table was way cool. It had a glass top, but there was a Gibson Les Paul guitar sticking up through the middle of the glass. The table held all kinds of music magazines. *Mix, Rolling Stone, Guitar Player, and some that said BMI.*

One wall was regular from the floor to about halfway up and then continued with solid glass. On the other side of the glass were all kinds of musical instruments.

"If this is my castle," Cory said, "then this room

is the moat. It keeps all the bad stuff out. Sorry guys, but the drinks stay out here."

"That's cool," I said.

Max nodded.

"Come on in." Cory opened a door to the right and took us into the control room.

I looked at Max. He slowly mouthed the word, "Impressive." His gaze darted all over the place. The whole room was full of stuff—real recording stuff.

My dad used to have a twelve-channel mixing board for his P.A. system. It was sort of like the one at school that Max volunteered to help with anytime we had an assembly.

Cory had two twenty-four-channel mixers. If he used all the channels, he could record four dozen people playing at the same time. Behind the mixers was another wall of glass looking into the big room with the instruments.

Cory sat in front of the controls and told Max to take the seat to his right.

"Don't let him touch anything," I said.

"Feedback? He'll be fine. I'll let him help a little. He'll be in charge of the drums. When I hear how many beats per minute you're playing, I'll set a metronome on the drum machine so you'll have something to help you keep time. I'll let Feedback press the start button."

"Oh, okay," I said even though I wasn't sure I knew what he was talking about.

"Don't worry. It won't be in the final mix, but you'll hear it while we record."

Cory got up and escorted me into the big room. "This is the live room, where the magic happens." He pressed a button on the wall, and the lights dimmed everywhere in the room except where we were standing.

"Do you want to sit or stand? I've known some studio musicians who can't play worth a flip when they stand. They say they've been playing sitting down for so long that they can't bend their wrist the right way to hit all the notes with their chord hand when they stand. That's why it's good to practice standing up if that's the way you're going to play."

"I'll stand," I said. "That's how I normally play." Cory handed me a cord to plug into my guitar.

"What kind of amp do you use?"

"I've got an old Fender. It just has one speaker."

"I'll plug you into a Fender Twin Reverb. I think you'll like it. Here are your headphones."

Cory handed me a set of the most expensive headphones I had ever seen, much less used.

I adjusted them while Cory walked back to the control room. Through the glass, I watched Max examine the knobs on the mixing boards. Cory handed him a set of headphones, and after reading everything printed on them, he put them on. Max must have been acting like an idiot again because both of them were laughing like crazy.

"Can you hear me, Rodney?" Cory's voice came through the headphones.

"Yeah," I answered, and then I looked around for a microphone. "Can you hear me?"

"Sure can," Max said. He was giving me two thumbs up and smiling like a kid with a new strawberry sucker. As much as he liked sound equipment, he had to be in heaven. Even if he didn't know a thing about recording.

"Okay, Rodney," Cory said, "go ahead and play something so I can adjust the levels. Let me know if it's loud enough or too loud for you."

I strummed an E minor chord. It sounded awesome through Cory's system.

"You serious?" Max's voice came through the headphones. "You're only going to play one chord?"

"It's just for a sound check," I told him.

"Okay," Cory said, "go ahead. Play something you want to record. I want to get the tempo."

I played a couple of notes, but my left hand wouldn't work right. My palm got all sweaty and was sticking to the guitar neck.

"You okay?" Cory asked.

"I think so. I guess my hand got hot. It's sweating."

"That happens. There's a towel on the back of the stool behind you and some hand wipes on the counter. Use them if you need."

He must be ready for anything, I thought. "Thanks." I used a hand wipe, dried my hand, then tried to play again, but I couldn't. It was almost like what happened at school. My face heated up, and the sushi swam around in my stomach.

"Okay, let's take a break," Cory said. He and Max removed their headphones and walked into the room with me. Cory flipped a switch in a box behind me, and then I could hear my guitar coming through the speakers in the room. He picked up a black Les Paul and plugged it into an amplifier on the other side of the room.

"Let's jam!" Cory smiled at me and winked at Max.

The next two hours were great. At first, all I wanted to do was listen to Cory and watch his hands. He was awesome. The best I had ever heard, and he made it look so easy. When I started to play, he began showing me stuff. I couldn't believe I was getting a guitar lesson from a real professional. He even let Max play a bongo drum. We sounded pretty good together.

I glanced at my watch. It was ten after nine. "We have to be going."

Max kept tapping on the little drum. I pointed toward the door. "Max, *we* gotta go."

I was trying to figure out how to ask if I could come back sometime when Cory asked, "Do you want to try again Tuesday evening?"

"Sure," I said and looked at Max. He smiled and nodded.

"Tuesday it is then," Cory added.

chapter FOUR

AFTER CHURCH ON SUNDAY, MOM MADE ME GO to town with her. Going to town consisted of checking out sales at the dollar store and going to Walmart.

"How'd it go at Cory's?" she asked. I think she liked to make me go shopping with her so we could talk. I was her captive audience, but that was okay. It was the only time we got to talk anymore.

"It was great," I said. "He's got an awesome setup. I heard you talking to Lenny from the Guitar Outlet on the phone about him. Thanks for checking him out."

Mom was weird about things like that. She worried about everything. For six months after she had seen a movie about some kid going missing, she wouldn't let me ride my bicycle out of the yard. I guess I couldn't blame her since it was just the two of us. We were all each other had. I couldn't imagine what it would be like if anything happened to her. I sure wouldn't want to have to live with Dad.

"I've got to look out for you, you know," she said.

"Did you have Jeff check him out on the police computers?" Jeff was sort of like her new boyfriend, though she would never admit it. She talked about him all the time, but when I'd ask, she'd say he was just a friend. He'd been with the Pigeon Forge Police Department for about ten years and spent a lot of time at the diner when Mom was working.

"You never know these days. Even your best friend could be an axe murderer."

"Cory would never hurt an axe," I said and laughed. "He loves guitars." I don't think she got the joke. I guess she didn't know that some musicians call a guitar an axe. She also never said if she had Jeff check out Cory.

"So, when are you two going out?"

Mom hadn't dated anyone since Dad got the bright idea to take off and become a professional musician. Once she told me she didn't have time for another man and that I was the only one she needed in her life. I didn't think it was because she still loved Dad, but more like she didn't want to get hurt again.

"Why should we go out? He has dinner with me at the diner almost every night." She laughed and pulled the car into a parking space at Walmart.

Inside, I went straight to the music section and looked for something by Cory Williams. I couldn't find anything. Next, I looked in the children's music and found a CD from the TV show *Safety Rulz*. Cory had written just about every song on it and had produced the whole CD.

Safety Rulz was a cool show. I used to watch it as a kid and loved the theme song. I'd never dreamed I would someday meet the person who wrote it.

When I looked in the classic rock section, I found *White Fire* by Bones. The back cover was the same as one of the pictures hanging on Cory's wall. It showed a young black man sitting on a train track, playing a guitar. In the background, you could see the caboose of a train as it was leaving.

The CD player in the car was busted, so I had to wait until I got home to play it. The whole *White Fire* CD was way cool. I couldn't believe I had never heard anything from it. While it was playing, I went online and Googled "*White Fire* CD."

The album had sold over five hundred thousand copies back when it first came out and had continued to sell a few thousand copies each year since.

One website had the photo from the back of the CD case. It was so huge I could see something that looked like a small bag hanging from the neck of Cory's guitar. Maybe he'd used a good luck charm, too. I did another search for "Bones guitar player good luck bag."

They say not to believe everything you find on the Internet, but it sure was interesting.

Cory "Bones" Williams (born Cory Harrison Williams July 26, 1949) is an American Blues/Blues Rock guitarist and singer-songwriter. Williams currently writes songs for Big Entertainment, a company that produces educational shows for children.

Early in his career, Williams was considered one of the greatest blues guitarists in the world. Most thought his career had ended when his wife left him in 1969. She took with her their two-year-old daughter, and he never saw them again.

The spotlight, whiskey, and a dice game cost him everything. In April of 1969, a drunken Cory Williams bet *his $65,000 home in a game of chance. Williams lost his home, family, and lifestyle, and dropped off the music radar.*

His battle with alcohol lasted several years. His health started to fail, and Williams knew he would have to give up the booze or give up his life. It is said that instead, he gave up his soul. On February 25, 1975, he made his way into Ridgecrest Cemetery in Memphis, Tennessee with a garden shovel and a pint of whiskey. It is in that cemetery that his idol and guitar teacher, the famous "Ole Joe (Blues) Mullins," was buried. When Williams emerged, he had mud on his knees and hands and was holding a small black bag with what was said to contain Ole Joe's finger bones. One month later Williams started his comeback tour with his new name—Bones—and the hit single "You Play the Game, You Pay the Price," which went to number one on the blues charts.

Again, Williams was on top of the world and kissed his blues good-bye when he signed with Big Entertainment. He says he has never looked back, but he did move back to his hometown of Pigeon Forge, Tennessee, where he writes and records music for three children's television shows.

I couldn't wait to tell Max. It was too late to call, so I emailed him the link.

As of Sunday night, the "Unplugged" count was at 5,421.

At school Monday morning, people were still making fun of me. The Guitar Outlet must have had a sale on air guitars over the weekend. Almost everyone in the hallway started playing one when I passed. Even Max when he met me at my locker. "So we have to go out and dig up some dead person and steal their finger bones?" Max asked.

"No, we're not digging anybody up. I just thought it was creepy that Cory would do something like that."

"The bag must have something to do with voodoo. According to the Internet anyway. I thought you had flipped out and wanted to do the same so you can play better to beat Eddie."

"Yeah, right. Where are we going to find the finger bones of a dead guitar player? Then we have to find some voodoo woman to cast a spell on them."

"We could get old Mrs. Fillmore. They say she's a witch."

"She's not a witch. She's just old."

"Maybe we can find a spell on the Internet to use," Max suggested.

"What about the bones?" I found my *Guitar Player* magazine and slammed the locker door.

"We might not need them. Maybe we can

borrow Cory's. I noticed a leather pouch in one of the display boxes on his showcase. It has to be his voodoo bag."

The bell rang, so we had to start another day at Mountain Side Middle.

I thought lunch period would never come. When Max sat down across the table from me, he pointed all his fingers in my direction and wiggled them. "Voodoo, voodoo, voodoo."

"What are you doing?" I asked. "You look silly."

"I'm putting a hex on you."

"I don't need a hex. I already can't play in front of people. I need a spell to make me not get nervous."

"Well, that's what I mean. It's a voodoo spell to make you a great guitar player."

"I can play already. Just not when people are watching." I poked something on my plate. "Are these chicken strips?"

"They're chicken *fingers*. Maybe we can use them for the voodoo spell." He held up one of the deep fried chicken pieces and wiggled it in a circle.

"You going to eat your roll? If not, I'll eat it for you. I'll trade you my peas."

I tossed my roll to him. "Keep the peas." The roll bounced off the piece of chicken he was waiving and landed in his mashed potatoes. My aim had never been anything to brag about.

Tuesday finally arrived. Cory surprised me with his old gig bag when we walked in. "I thought you could use this," he said. "Sorry about the stains, but it is clean. I thought it might come in handy for you on that bicycle. That sleeping bag must be a mess to use."

"Wow! Thanks." It even had a strap so I wouldn't have to use the bungee cord anymore.

We made our way down to the studio.

"I thought we'd jam for a few minutes before we get started," Cory said.

"Okay, great," I said. I figured he was trying to get me to relax again. It worked. We played three songs together, and then he played a song he'd written for one of the kid's shows. I couldn't keep up with him.

Cory and Max took their places in the control room. "Okay, everyone ready?" Cory asked.

"I'm ready with the beats," Max said. He smiled and held his finger above the start button on the drum sequencer.

I nodded and let the tap of an electronic drumstick hitting the rim of an electronic snare drum count me in. *Click, click, click, click.* Amazed at how real it sounded, I closed my eyes and played. It was awesome. My guitar sounded smooth, almost liquid—if liquid could be considered a sound.

"That was good," Cory said when I finished. He smiled at Max and gave him a high five. "Want to try it again?"

"Sure, this is fun." I nodded and waited for the click track. He recorded my song two more times, and then I played a rhythm track along with each version.

"Ready to listen?" Cory asked.

"Yeah," I said.

Cory motioned for me to come into the control room. "Take a right at the top of the stairs," he was saying to Max as I walked in. "It's the first door on the left."

"Potty time," Max said and rushed out.

I took a seat beside Cory and watched as he

pushed buttons on the control board. The sound of my guitar filled the room. It sounded like something from a real CD.

"It's different," I said.

"I added a couple of effects. A little chorus and a touch of delay. I can change it if you don't like it, but it's how I usually set it for my stuff."

"No, it's great. I love it. It sounds better than I do," I said. And it did.

"Think of it like a supermodel. She's already beautiful, but they still put makeup on her and Photoshop away the flaws."

"Do you have something to take the flaws away when I miss a note?"

"That's called punching in. You play along with the first track we record, and then, when you get to the bad notes, I punch you in and record the new notes in place of the old ones. So if you ever mess up while we're recording, just keep playing. We'll fix it."

"How about something to help when I'm playing live? When my fingers don't work." I looked at my palms then folded my hands on my lap.

"That's called practice. I know some guitar players who are great in the studio, but get nervous on stage. Now they do make something for singers.

Sometimes if you can't hear yourself because of a bad monitor mix when you're singing live, you can go off key. They make a unit that digitally corrects your pitch so your vocals sound perfect on every note. Just ain't fair for us musicians, but that's the way the mop flops."

Max came back in with Myra Fredricks from school. "Look who I found."

"Hey, girl," Cory said. "Where's my hug?"

Myra walked over and hugged Cory. "Boys, this is my niece, Myra. Well, technically she's my great-niece, but who's counting? She's trying to teach an old dog some new tricks." Myra handed Cory a stack of papers. He held up a page of handwritten sheet music in each hand. Someone had circled some of the notes with red ink. "After all these years, I'm learning to read and transcribe music—from an eighth grader. I write out my songs, and she corrects them. I'm getting better at it." He turned to Myra. "I just finished a new batch, so don't let me forget to give them to you when you're ready to leave."

Myra was probably the smartest person in my history class. She really got sparks going when we studied anything about slavery or Native Americans. One day, she asked the teacher how people could come to America and take land from the Native Americans, then go to another country and capture people to bring back and make them slaves, then stick up the Statue of Liberty and call America the land of the free.

"She's been taking piano lessons since fourth grade," Cory said. "I taught her the Nashville Number System, so if you need keyboards, you might get her to record some tracks."

"Cool," I said. "I think it would sound good with an organ."

"That sounds like fun." Myra played a silent keyboard riff in the air.

"She's always looking for a chance to record," Cory added.

"I'll play the drums," Max said. "I'm getting pretty good at pressing the start button." He wriggled his pointer finger and poked his nose twice as if he were trying to get it to do something.

We all laughed. Cory played my guitar tracks again for Myra and Max. "I think we're finished for today, but if you can come back Saturday, we'll record the keyboards. I'll chart it out for Myra."

Dad had taught me the Nashville Number System a few years ago. At first I thought he was crazy, but then it started making sense. You can take any song and play it in any key if you have it charted out by the chord number. And you don't have to be able to read music.

I couldn't wait for history class on Wednesday. I would finally have an excuse to talk to Myra.

chapter
FIVE

THE OFFICIAL "UNPLUGGED" COUNT ON
Wednesday morning was 6,789.

When I walked into history class, Eddy and
Myra were laughing about something but got all
quiet when they saw me.

"Hi, Myra." I gave a quick wave as I passed
them. When she tried to wave back, she dropped
her books and pages of sheet music went
everywhere.

"Hey there, Rodney," Eddie said then stooped
to help pick up the papers. "Myra, have you seen
Rodney's 'Unplugged' video?"

I made it to my seat two desks back.

"No, I didn't know he had one," she said.

"Give me your email address, and I'll send you the link," Eddie said.

What a lame way to get a girl's email address, I thought. I wished I could have found a video of him messing up or embarrassing himself or something. I doubted anything like that actually existed since he was "Mr. Perfect."

I had hoped to get to talk to Myra, but it looked like they were having too much fun, so I tried to find the page we were on in my history book. I couldn't help listening to them, though. They giggled and chatted until all the papers were picked up. When I found chapter thirteen, I scanned to find something familiar.

"Rodney," Myra said. My face heated up when she spoke to me.

"Yeah?"

"I worked out the keyboard parts to your song so we can record on Saturday. I hope you like them."

"Wow. Thanks for helping out." I couldn't believe she came back just to talk to me.

I looked up and saw that Eddie had gone to his desk. He was pretending his right forearm was a guitar neck and fingering guitar chords with his left hand. I guess he was off in his own world because he was swaying to a song only he could hear.

After class was over, I had no idea what the teacher had said. All I could think about was recording at Cory's—and Myra.

"You've got to come over after school," Max said at lunch. "You'll never guess what I found online."

"My video with a million hits?"

"No, I found real voodoo spells. Look, I printed some." He handed me a folder he had put together with all kinds of weird stuff in it. "But we gotta watch out for the power of return."

"What in the flip is that?" I asked.

"Can I have your roll?" He reached a hand across the table and hovered it over the dinner roll.

"What's the power of return thing?" I grabbed the roll and held it above my head.

"It's like if something backfires with the spell, it can return to us and do three times as much bad as what good it was supposed to do."

"That's wild," I said. I threw the roll at him, but it bounced off the edge of the table and rolled across the floor. "Guess we don't have to worry about that since we don't have any dead fingers to work with."

"That's why you have to come over. I have a surprise." He slinked from his chair and retrieved the roll.

"You got a voodoo lady hidden in your bedroom?"

"No, something better." He brushed off the roll and laid it on his plate. "It's a surprise." He gave me a corny smile and two thumbs up. "Did you know it's bad luck to burn a spider? There's a bunch of superstitions in there, too." He reached over and started flipping to the back pages. "And you should never shake a left hand. Or pull a feather off a buzzard while it's sleeping."

"You're the official voodoo information network now," I said. "Have you found a spell to cure rigor mortis?"

"You mean to bring back the dead?"

"No. One to make me not freeze up so I can play." I glanced toward the lunch line where Eddie was playing drums on his milk carton with two celery sticks.

"Well, I think we'll have to combine a couple of them."

"Do we have to make a voodoo doll and stick

pins in it and all that stuff?" *I'll name mine Eddie*, I thought.

"No, but we do have to go into a graveyard at midnight," Max said. "That's where my surprise comes in."

chapter
six

"I DIDN'T REALLY STEAL IT," MAX SAID. "I JUST borrowed it."

"What do you mean you didn't steal it? It's here in your room, and it's not yours. What will Cory do when he notices it's missing?"

"He won't. I put another bag in its place. It looks exactly like this one—almost. It was kind of like in that old Indiana Jones movie." Max mimed picking up a bag with one hand as he rolled his other hand over to drop something in its place.

"So, what do we do with it?" I picked up the little black bag to examine. The leather was soft. It was almost like the felt we used in third grade art class to make turkeys for Thanksgiving, except it was smooth. It had a faded yellow drawstring, but was sewn shut. "It has a box inside."

"Yeah, and if you shake it, you can hear the finger bones rattle around."

I threw the bag onto his desk. "Yuck! That's just creepy. He must have had awful short fingers."

"Maybe it's knuckle bones or something," Max said with a shrug. "I've heard of pig's knuckles. Some people eat them."

"So now we just figure out which spells we want to use, right?" I said. "They're hundreds of them. How do we know which ones to choose?"

Max flipped through the folder until he came to a page with my name on it. "I've already taken care of it. I printed extra copies for us to study and get stuff together." He pulled some pages out and read to himself.

I thumbed through the rest of the folder. There were spells for just about anything you could think of. Even one to help get rid of zits on your face and, well, other parts of your body.

"It says we can adjust the words for our own personal needs," Max said. "We also have to get a purple candle, a piece of cedar wood, some black tea, a lemon, some rose oil, incense, and a mirror.

Then we have to find a freshly dug grave, and around midnight, we read these words while we mix everything with the fresh dirt from the grave."

"Let me see." I snatched the page he was holding. "Wow, we actually have to go into a graveyard at midnight?"

"Yep," Max said. "You, me, and that bag of bones."

"I don't know about this," I said. "What were you saying about the power of return earlier today?" I couldn't believe we were actually talking voodoo, cemeteries, and grave dirt.

"Well, that's only if something goes wrong. Then the spell can come back to you three times as bad."

"So if this backfires, I may not be able to play at all?"

"Nothing is going to go wrong," Max said. "How could it?"

"Well, since we don't know what we're doing, a lot could go wrong. Where in the world are we going to find a fresh grave?"

"Duh." Max smacked his forehead with his palm. "Maybe in a graveyard?"

"I know that." I shoved the folder across the

desk. "I mean, what are we going to do, read the obituaries every day until someone dies?"

"Pretty much." Max nodded. "We'll have to wait 'til someone is buried in one of the cemeteries close-by."

"I guess my fate as a guitar player depends on someone in the neighborhood kickin' the bucket before the contest. What if it's someone we know? We can't go out at midnight and start digging around in their grave. That's too weird."

"Well, you could forfeit the contest and let Eddie win." He shoved the folder back at me. Guess he knew I was ready to try anything.

I pretended to hold a phone to my ear. "Hello. Is this a funeral home? Okay, good. I was wondering if you just might have a dead body you're going to be burying in Mountain Side Cemetery any time soon. Well, if you get one, could you give me a call?"

"Yeah, I can get you all the phone numbers," Max said.

"We would sound like a couple of idiots. Who calls funeral homes to ask where their stiffs are going to be buried?"

"Well, at least we'll have time to get everything

together so we can be ready to go. Maybe we should check out the graveyard in daylight. That way we'll know our way around."

"Yeah, and I'll draw us a map. We can memorize the names of all the dead people from the gravestones so we know exactly where we're going."

"That would be great," Max said.

"It's just a big square, doofus." I drew a huge square in the air with my finger. "Why do we need to check it out? It's not like we're going to get lost or anything."

"Well, I thought it would be a good idea to be prepared. Just in case."

Sometimes Max could get carried away with things. He would make a great teacher someday. He was always so organized.

"So, we write this up in our own words?" I asked, looking at the page with the spells on it.

"Yeah. You just follow the sample and fill in what you want the spell to cover."

"That's it? That's all we have to do?"

He made it sound way too easy. I rewrite the spell and it would banish my stage fright forever. Max would gather all the stuff we needed to perform the ceremony. He let me borrow the folder of witchcraft and magic with voodoo and superstitions thrown in. I would have to sneak it in without Mom seeing the big goat-headed picture of Baphomet Max had pasted on the front, or she would flip out. She didn't mind me playing rock, but she said some of the stuff I liked sounded like devil music. There were only a few bands she wouldn't let me listen to. I didn't mind. I didn't listen to rock to make a statement or protest parents like a lot of kids that I knew did. I listened because I liked the music. Especially the guitars.

After dinner, I went to my room to check out the paper Max had given me with the spell on it. Since we would have to wait until we could find a fresh grave, I figured I'd have a day or two to come up with something. I looked at some of the other spells and thought they would be like stuff from horror movies, but most of them were just silly. Then, I looked for something to make Myra like me more. I found a love spell but thought it might be a little much. Even though she was fun to be with and wasn't bad to look at, I decided to try one for friendship. I would just have to burn a pink candle and chant her name.

I put the spell paper back in the folder and buried it under a blanket in the corner of my closet.

By bedtime, the "Unplugged" count was up to 7,664.

chapter SEVEN

THURSDAY MORNING, MAX MET ME AT MY locker. "You'll never guess what I found when I was fixing Einstein's newspaper this morning." He whispered like he was keeping a highly classified secret.

"Your dog reads the newspaper?" I asked.

"No, we're paper-training him. It's for him to go potty on." He held out a rolled-up section of the *Mountain Side Daily*. "Guess what's in it." He offered the paper to me, but I declined and backed up against the lockers.

"Dog poop?"

"No, it's Tuesday's obituary. Tommy Jefferies died on Monday. He gets buried today in Mountain Side Cemetery. Tonight's the night."

"Wow." I never expected anyone to die so soon. Did it happen so we would have a fresh grave? "Do you think he died because of us?"

"He was ninety-eight years old. It must have been his time. Mrs. Jefferies always said he was going to drink himself to death. Guess he finally did."

I had the rest of the day to figure out how to sneak out of the house without Mom finding out. At lunch, Max and I worked out a timeline counting backward from midnight. I had to be out no later than 10:34.

Mountain Side Cemetery looked completely different at night. Especially from inside the fence. We walked on a worn path through the center of the graveyard. A rumble of thunder in the distance made me wonder if we should have brought an umbrella.

"This is a bad omen," I said.

"No, It's just thunder," Max said. "Maybe it's because of what you put in your spell." He stretched his arms out to his sides and looked to the sky. "Think of all the positives. Old man

Jefferies died, it's a full moon, and we have the bones."

"I don't think dying is a positive."

"Well, not for Mr. Jefferies, but for us. You know what I mean."

"I wonder where they put him." I guess I should have listened to Max about scouting the place out. We would have seen where they had dug the new grave. It was a full moon, but that just made everything look more eerie. The only lights were three miles away on the Parkway in Pigeon Forge. The giant Ferris wheel made the city look like a miniature carnival inside a snow globe. Of all the things that were on the list to bring, neither of us remembered a flashlight. If we'd had a screwdriver, we could have removed the lights from our bicycles.

The moonlight gave the graveyard a gray tint. I couldn't help thinking about the old "Thriller" video by Michael Jackson that's on TV each Halloween.

"Rodney," Max whispered, "over there." He pointed toward a grave with flowers all over it.

"Stop whispering. You're creeping me out. Nobody is going to hear us."

"It helps set the mood so we can get into the spirit."

"This ain't Christmas, and I think the mood is setting itself."

When we got to the gravesite, I pulled the folded paper I had written my spell on out of my pocket. Max moved some of the flowers out of the way and pulled up a square chunk of grass that had been placed on top of the fresh dirt.

"Hold this," Max said and handed me a pencil.

"What's it for?"

"We have to use a stick of cedar. That's the wood most pencils are made from. You can tell by the smell. The good smelling ones are cedar."

I sniffed the pencil.

"I figure it won't hurt to make some substitutions as long as they contain the ingredients the spell calls for." Max dug some other stuff out of his backpack. "Use it to draw a circle in the dirt. Go ahead."

I drew the circle. It wasn't perfect, but it was a circle. Max lit a purple birthday candle and dripped some wax onto a small round mirror. He stuck the bottom of the candle into the hot wax until it cooled, then blew out the flame.

"Cool candleholder," I said.

When he placed it in the middle of the circle, I could see the reflection of the moon in it. He scooped up some loose dirt from the grave and dumped it into a small silver bowl. I wondered if he had gone to a witch supply store and bought a special container for mixing eye of newt and stuff like that.

"Where'd that come from?" I asked.

"It's Einstein's."

"You brought your dog's food bowl?"

"No. It's his water bowl. He'll never miss it. He has three more. Mom sticks them everywhere so he doesn't get dehydrated."

Things were getting creepier by the minute. And darker. Clouds were starting to cover the moon. After Max finished adding and mixing stuff in Einstein's bowl, it smelled like a giant lemon drop. He lit a match then checked his notes.

"Okay, it's almost fifteen minutes 'til midnight." He shook the match to extinguish it. "When I say *now*, we light the candle."

We didn't say anything for about two minutes while Max watched the glowing dial of his watch. The air even started to feel weird. A breeze would blow, and it was like someone turning the thermostat up and down. First, it was warm, and then it would feel cool. After a few seconds, it would get warm again.

"It's fifteen 'til," Max said. "Time to start." He struck another match and lit the candle.

"Why fifteen 'til?" I asked. "I thought we were supposed to do it at midnight."

"Midnight is the time between good magic and evil magic. Fifteen 'til is the time to start because we're doing good magic. According to hoodoo anyway."

"Hoodoo? I thought we were doing voodoo."

"We're using a little of both, I guess. Okay, get ready to start reading."

Max dripped rose oil onto the dirt mixture in the bowl.

"Give me the pencil." He pulled a goldfish-shaped sharpener out of his backpack and used it on the pencil, letting the shavings drop into the mixture. He handed me a stick of incense. "Okay, now light this."

I held it over the candle to light.

"Blow it out!" Max said.

When I did, the end of the stick glowed red and started to smolder. "That stinks. What scent is it? Rotten gym socks?"

"It's Dragon's Blood." Max took the smoking stick and stuck it into the ground beside the bowl. "Now read your paper."

I had to lie down and hold my paper up to the candle to see the words. It was supposed to be a spell, but it sounded more like a poem to me. Max dangled the voodoo bag above the candle as I read.

"With power like a raging storm,

"Expel my fears when I perform.

"Let my music freely flow,

"From deep within my bones and soul."

In the distance, I saw flashes of lightning. The clouds were getting thicker. And blacker.

"Keep reading," Max said.

"This is creepy." My hands started to tremble.

"With power from both night and day,

"Pass confidence of song my way.

"I take control of all my fear,

"To play the tunes that all may hear."

When I spoke the last word, there was an instantaneous flash of lightning and clap of thunder. The spell must have started working because nature was already showing us the power of both night and day. Alternating between dark and light—with sound effects.

The lightning was like someone taking your picture with a flash camera six inches in front of your eyeballs so you couldn't see anything for a few seconds. Everything went black. Slowly, as my sight returned, I could see the faint glow of the candle. Max and I looked at each other for a second. Then we both burst out laughing.

"What was that all about?" Max asked.

"I guess we're doing something right, but this is creeping me out."

"Looks like it got the power lines." He pointed to where the city lights had been before. "It took out all of Pigeon Forge."

The candle sizzled and went out when a solitary drop of rain fell. Everything went dark. Then, with another simultaneous flash of lightning and crack of thunder, the clouds above opened up and dumped a monsoon on us.

chapter EIGHT

GYM CLASS ON FRIDAY STARTED ALMOST SEVEN days to the minute from when I had taken the stage for the talent show. Coach Brown must have had better things to do because he assigned us to teams and made us play half court basketball while he went to his office.

CRACK! I grabbed my right index finger and dropped to my knees. Everything started spinning, and my lunch wanted to come back up. I guess those fire safety lessons from the second grade kicked in, because since I had already stopped and dropped, I decided to start rolling around like an idiot.

"Dude," Max said, "you okay?"

When I was able to breathe again I slowly

uncurled my hand from around my finger. "It's broken."

"How can a basketball break your finger?"

"I don't know. Get the coach."

Max ran across the gym floor yelling, "Coach Brown! Rodney's dying!"

The whole class huddled around me to get a look at my finger. The swelling made it hurt too much to move.

"Too bad," Eddie said. "There goes your guitar career. Oh, I forgot; you don't play anyway."

"He's faking to get out of gym class," Billy Johnson said.

"Okay, boys," Coach Brown said, shooing them away, "take five." The coach shook his head when he looked at my hand. "Guess we need to get you to the nurse's office before it pops. It looks pretty bad."

That's all I needed to hear. The contest was less than a month away, and I got a broken finger.

Nurse Pam was trying to calm some whiny seventh grader. From what I could hear, she had gotten her knee scraped when someone—she wouldn't tell who —tripped her out on the sidewalk.

After what seemed like forever, Nurse Pam called my name. Just in time, too, because I was ready to shove the whiny girl out the door of the nurse's office.

"We need to call your mom and get you to the clinic for an X-ray," Nurse Pam said. "You'll be lucky if it isn't broken."

I guess I was lucky. I got to skip school, ride with NASCAR driver wannabe Nurse Pam, and sit in pain for another half hour at the clinic.

They called my name, and I got to go through the weights and measures department. Then they checked my temperature and blood pressure. I wondered how long it would take them to realize I had a hurt finger.

Some girl took me to get an X-ray. She must have had too much radiation exposure because the first thing she said was, "Does it hurt?"

After she finished with me, she put me in a room for more waiting. When Dr. Sanders came in, she stuck the X-ray film to a box on the wall with a light in it. She pointed to my finger bones where I was hurt. They looked cool. Then she showed me a model of a skeleton's hand with the muscles still attached. She pointed to two of the finger bones and explained what I had done.

"It's not broken," she said. "It's just jammed, but it is going to hurt for a while." She went to work on me like she had fixed nine hundred ninety-nine thousand, nine hundred and ninety-nine fingers before mine. I wondered what I might win for being her millionth customer.

"How long do I have to wear this thing?" I held up my prize. She had stuck some kind of splint made of aluminum and cushy foam around my finger.

"Maybe just a couple of weeks. It usually takes two to six weeks to heal. After that, you should be good as new."

"But I've got a talent show coming up. I won't be able to hold my guitar pick with this thing on."

"You'll just have to take it easy and let it heal. It'll be sore for a while, so let it rest."

Mom picked me up at the clinic, and on our way home, she stopped at the diner and came out with two to-go boxes. Who needed to stock a refrigerator when we could get all the free food we wanted?

Max rode his bike over after school. I'm not sure if he came to help me or torture me.

"Maybe we can duct tape a guitar pick to the end of the splint," Max said. "Or I've got some Super Glue that might work."

I had duct tape in my desk left over from my science project. We sat on my bed while Max worked on the splint. Sometimes his wild ideas sounded like they might work. That one didn't. The duct tape was too flimsy to hold the pick. Not to mention that every time I strummed, it felt like my finger was being ripped off.

"This won't work," I said. "I'll never be able to do this. Guess Eddie wins." I tugged at the pick dangling from the splint. It wouldn't budge.

"Just tell yourself it doesn't hurt. You know, like hypnosis or something."

"Yeah, right. Let me break your finger, and you tell yourself it doesn't hurt." I grabbed for one of his fingers with my left hand but missed. He was too fast.

"You said it wasn't broken."

I gave him one of Mom's squinty-eyed stares. "I know, but it hurts just the same. I can't play, and there's nothing I can do about it. Just leave it alone. I'll withdraw from the contest."

I guess he was disappointed I wouldn't let him torture me anymore, because he went home.

How could you tell yourself that you couldn't feel something and believe it?

Later that night, I had the wild idea to go back to the graveyard and try some kind of voodoo spell to fix my finger. I flipped through the Baphomet folder, but it started to creep me out again. I shoved it back under the blanket.

I guess the pain medicine helped some, but I fell asleep before my finger stopped hurting. I even forgot to check the hits on my video.

chapter
NINE

I NEVER KNEW HOW BORING LIFE COULD BE without being able to play music. It didn't take long to realize that it sucked. Bad! I wondered how people lived. Maybe all those video games kept them busy. Mom told me I had to put ice on my finger like they showed me at the clinic. Every hour, I froze my finger for twenty minutes. She also told me I couldn't go to Cory's if it didn't feel better. I didn't think it was a lie to tell her that it did because it *did* feel better than when it first happened. She let me go.

Riding my bicycle was rough, especially when I had to grip the handlebars hard to pull the hills, but it was worth it. I wasn't going to miss hearing Myra putting the keyboard parts to my song.

Cory must have been waiting for me, because as soon as I stepped up to the door, it opened. "Hello, Rodney." He glanced over to my bike, then back to me. "Where's your guitar?"

"I had a little accident." I held up my splinted finger.

"Oh, my. What's that?"

"It's not broken, but I can't play. It hurts too much." I explained my basketball adventure, which bought enough time to glance over at Max's voodoo bag. It actually looked like the real one.

"Go on down. I'll be there in a minute."

"Hey, Rodney, you made it," Max said when I walked into the control room.

"Hi, Rodney." Myra's voice came through the monitor speakers.

I hadn't noticed her sitting in the back corner of the live room at one of the keyboards.

"Okay," Cory said from behind me, "everyone ready?" He walked in, took his seat, handed me a set of headphones, and started the recording.

After four beats of the click track, a band started playing my song. Cory had put drums in place of the clicks and added a bass guitar. When Myra started playing, my insides melted. It was like my song was a *real* song. Myra closed her eyes and swayed to the music. There wasn't a lot of light in the room, but enough to see how...well, how good she could play.

"Are you with us?" Cory asked. "Rodney? Hey, you okay, boy?"

"Yeah." I jumped at the sound of my own voice. At least it snapped me out of the spell she had me under. A surge of heat rushed across my face. "I must have zoned out. Getting into the music, I guess."

The music had stopped, but I hadn't noticed.

"Mesmerizing, huh, Rodney?" Cory asked.

"Yeah, she...I mean, sounds great." I couldn't think straight. Max was acting like an idiot again, puckering his lips behind his hands so Myra couldn't see.

"Was that okay, Rodney?" Myra asked.

"Yeah, that was great."

"Rest your finger bones a minute and we'll try it again," Cory said.

Myra removed her headphones and came out of the live room. "Rodney, you sure it was okay?"

"It was great." I couldn't believe she was even asking me. It was like having a professional keyboard player laying down tracks on my song.

"It's fine, Myra," Cory said, "but we need to

record at least two more. You were just warming up. I firmly believe in the rule of three. Record at least three takes and go with the best. Sometimes we tend to put more feelings into the later ones. We get in the groove."

He knows. Why else would he say anything about the rule of threes? Like Max was talking about with the power of return coming back three times if the spell backfired. I did three takes, but he never mentioned anything about it.

I felt sushi gut coming on again.

"Can I have a Pepsi, Cory?" I thought it might help my stomach.

"Sure. Help yourself. You know where they are. Just keep it out there." He pointed to the moat room.

"Anyone else want anything?"

I felt like Mom taking orders at the diner, except I didn't have one of those little pads to write on. No one answered. They were all too busy getting ready to record another track.

I waited in the moat room while Myra finished the keyboards for the second take. Cory turned on the monitor speakers so I could hear everything. Each time Myra played, it sounded smoother than the last. I guess that's what Cory had meant about getting in the groove.

"You okay out there, Rodney?" Cory asked.

"Yeah, guess my pain medicine made me a little queasy." I was glad I hadn't thrown up on the equipment in the control room. "I'll be fine."

"I think we've done enough for today," Cory said after Myra finished the third recording. "I'm going to put on my producer's hat and call for another keyboard track. I think Myra needs to add a piano track. How about we try again Tuesday?"

I couldn't think about anything but Myra during the ride back home. Well, at least until the monsoon hit again. I guess my finger was a sacrifice so the rain didn't soak through the gig bag and ruin my guitar. That's what would have happened if I had brought it. By the time I got home, I was waterlogged.

chapter
TEN

"He's stupid! He knows I'm supposed to play in the guitar competition. It's not my fault he lost his guitar in a poker game. Why does he even still have a house key?"

"Rodney, that's enough," Mom said, walking out of the kitchen.

"No, it's not enough, Mom. It's not enough that he takes off and leaves us, and then comes and goes when he pleases. Now he gets to take things back that he gave us, too?" I don't know where the courage came from to say what I did, but I couldn't hold it in any longer. I stood dripping in the middle of the living room.

"He's stupid," I added.

"He's still your dad."

"That's your fault. Maybe you were stupid, too."

"Maybe I was." She stopped about a foot in front of me, hands on her hips, and gave me her famous glare. "Maybe I was stupid for not leaving you with your granny and traipsing off with him on his 'gonna be a star' dream. Maybe I'm stupid for thinking I could raise you by myself. God knows he ain't any help. And from the looks of it, you're going to be just like him."

"Mom, I'll never—"

"Music is all either one of you cares about. All you ever do when you're here is close yourself in that room of yours and play that stupid guitar he gave you. Maybe it's a good thing he took it. Maybe I'll at least get to see you when you're not out with Max or over at Cory's. Now get in there and get out of those wet clothes."

"I'll never be like him," I yelled as I ran to my room.

I sat on my bed and stared at the poster.

I couldn't believe I'd called Mom stupid. I had never thought about it, but maybe she did still love Dad. I knew I was supposed to love him and all, but sometimes I wasn't sure how I felt about him.

How can you make yourself feel something when you don't?

I stared at the rabbit's foot on the poster and wondered if it was the power of return causing bad things to happen. Something must have gone wrong with the spell. My finger was messed up, Dad took my guitar, and Mom might still be in love with him. I wished I had kept the guitar in the gig bag instead of putting it back in its case.

As I pulled Cory's voodoo bag from my pocket, I heard the bones rattle inside. It had worked for him. He was a success and could have anything he wanted. All he had to do was sit around and make music. Why did my spell have to backfire?

I pulled Baphomet from under the blanket in the closet. It wasn't like I was looking for some customer support website or phone number. I just wanted to know what to do when things went wrong. Of all the chants and spells and superstitions Max had found, there was nothing to cancel what we had done. Baphomet was no help at all. I was on my own.

I imagined going to Cory and telling him we stole his voodoo bag and something went wrong. Now I needed his help. I could see him waving the bag in front of me, laughing and saying, "It's the power of return, kid. You play the game, you pay the price."

The knock on my door startled me. "Rodney, time to eat," Mom said.

I stuck the folder back in the closet, then changed clothes and went to the table. Sometimes the food Mom brought home was a surprise. Mom's boss, Johnny, always let her bring home free to-go boxes. I think he liked helping us out since money was tight and he knew what a bum Dad was. I never knew what to expect until I opened the Styrofoam box. Most of the time, it was good. Sometimes it was weird. She knew what I liked, but sometimes she'd put broccoli or green beans in because they were good for me.

"Mom." My voice cracked. "I didn't mean to call you stupid. I was just mad at Dad. He knows I have the contest coming up and I need a guitar."

"I'm sorry for what I said, too. I get so aggravated at him sometimes. He's got it made. He does whatever he wants, whenever he wants to. We're the ones stuck trying to survive day to day. Who wouldn't want to live his life and just run away from it all and not have to worry about anything? I'm not wired that way. I love you and would never leave you for anything. You just made me mad. I know it's my fault you have the father you do, but if it weren't for him, you wouldn't be you."

"I know, but he *is* a jerk."

She sat the Styrofoam containers on the table and pulled her chair closer to me. "We're trying a new dish at the diner."

"Oh, God." The last time she told me they were trying something new, she had put a dead mouse, still in the trap, on a leaf of lettuce. It had ketchup dripped all over it along with some green gooey stuff. My Halloween dinner.

I put my hand on the lid to keep her from opening it. "Only if you promise to take the first bite."

"It's for real. No jokes. It's real food. I'll eat the first bite."

I moved my hand, and she unsnapped the latch on the lid. The top bounced up just enough for me to peek inside. "Mom! Yuck!"

She laughed. "That's how they cook them."

"Well, next time tell Johnny to cut the head off. I don't like fish looking back at me. What is it?"

"Rainbow Trout. Something new he'd wanted to try. Go on. It's good."

"Maybe this summer, Johnny will pay me to fish for him. Now that would be a cool job. Get paid for fishing. It would have to be easier than mowing the lawn for Ms. Lane next door." Mom worked a lot just so we could make it, but I wished I had a real job so I could help. The prize money from the guitar competition wouldn't hurt either.

Dinner turned out okay. We could never stay mad at each other for long. I still wondered, though, if she ever wished I wasn't around so she could be free like Dad. I'd always wonder about that, but I knew she would never leave me.

Maybe I could find a spell for Mom. One that would make her happy with the life she had. Maybe we wouldn't argue as much.

chapter
ELEVEN

I PULLED MY OLD GUITAR CASE FROM THE BACK OF my closet. It looked like something some wannabe carpenter tried to put together. It was dangerous. You could get a splinter from it. Someone had made it out of rough plywood and painted it orange with big white letters that said, "Go Vols!" The paint was flaking off in big chunks. It had thick foam padding on the inside. I guess it worked because the only thing that ever got damaged when I took it anywhere was my pride. At least I had the gig bag that Cory had given me.

The guitar felt good, and the strap was in good shape too. I wouldn't have to worry about it coming off the strap button. I hadn't messed with it for about two years, and it sounded awful. The strings were rusty and had something crusted all over them. I tried holding a pick between my middle finger and thumb, but it was awkward.

I took the splint off and tried some fancy finger picking Dad had taught me. It didn't help. It was hard not to use my index finger. I was doing okay, but the pain was too much if I wiggled it even a little.

Every time I bent a string or used the whammy bar, the guitar would go out of tune. Even if my finger wasn't hurt, there was no way I could get through a whole song unless I was just strumming rhythm. How can you play the blues and not bend strings? I thought about bottleneck slide, but that was a completely different style. Every time I had tried, I sucked. Too much noise. Besides, I only had two weeks until the competition, and there was no way I could have learned anything worth playing.

I stuck the splint back on and went to the living room to ask Mom to take me to the Guitar Outlet for new strings. She handed me a letter from the Music Today Theater in Pigeon Forge.

"Why didn't you give me this when I first came home?"

"Well, it may have something to do with the

way you were calling everyone stupid and the fit you threw. You better be glad I remembered it at all."

I took the letter to the kitchen table to read. It was my confirmation packet with a release form for Mom to sign so I could participate. It also informed me I had to be at the theater by 10:00 a.m. on Saturday. I didn't realize when I signed up for the competition that I would have to audition. I had a week to get ready.

"Mom!" I stormed back into the living room. "You've got to take me to the Guitar Outlet. I have to get my old guitar ready by Saturday. It needs strings. Bad."

"Saturday? I thought the show was in two weeks."

"It is, but the auditions are next Saturday." I threw the letter onto the table. "I hate Dad."

"Rodney! What's gotten into you? Haven't we fought this fight enough today?"

"Well, he messes up everything. If my finger hadn't been hurt, I would have had my good guitar with me, and he couldn't have taken it. Why now?"

"Because that's what your father is good for. Finding the best time to do the worst things." She turned and glared at me. "You better not grow up to be like him. You can play your music all you want to, but if you ever start treating people like he does, I don't know what I'll do to you, but I'll do something."

"Will you take me? Please? If it wasn't raining, I'd ride my bike."

"I don't know why I should. Didn't you just buy strings last Saturday?"

"They're in the guitar case Dad took."

She turned to walk away. "Get in the car. I'll be there in a minute."

I grabbed the plywood guitar case and ran to the car.

"You have to have the whole guitar with you to buy strings?" she asked when she saw the case on the back seat.

"No, but I need Lenny to look at it. I think it needs something adjusted."

We got to the Guitar Outlet ten minutes before they closed. I jumped out of the car, grabbed the case, and ran inside.

"Hi, Rodney," Lenny said. "How you doing?"

"Not too good. I messed up my finger, Dad took my guitar, and I have to audition for the guitar competition using this thing." I put the case on the floor and opened the latches.

"Wow," Lenny said. "What's that?"

"It's an old Strat copy Dad gave me years ago. It doesn't have a brand name or logo on it. It's kinda lame"—I shrugged—"but it's all I have."

"Looks like you need strings. How's it play?"

"The action is good, but it won't stay in tune when I bend a string or use the whammy bar. I was hoping you could do something."

"I don't have anything here, but you need to block up the tremolo."

"What's that mean?"

"You wedge a block of wood in between the tremolo system and the body. You won't be able to use your whammy bar anymore, but it won't go out of tune as often."

I bought the strings and wondered if I would be able to find something to fix it with.

When I got home, I searched the Internet for stuff about blocking the tremolo system on a Stratocaster. Of all the junk we had around the house, I couldn't find a single piece of wood to use. I considered taking the plywood guitar case apart to see if I could use part of it, but I didn't have a hammer or a saw since Dad took all his tools with him. I called Max. He said he would see what he could come up with.

chapter TWELVE

MONDAY MORNING, I MET MAX IN FRONT OF THE school when his mom dropped him off. He pulled a piece of wood from his backpack. "Watch the nail," he said.

The rusty nail looked like a crooked witch's finger. The whole thing reminded me of something from Farmer Green's barn down the road from the house. "It's a little long, don't you think?"

"You said you needed a piece of wood. It's the shortest piece I could find."

I held the board up by the nail. "Now I'll need a tetanus shot. Who do you know with a saw?"

"Why?"

"I can't have a two-foot board sticking out of the back of my guitar."

Max stuffed the thing back into his backpack. "Mitchell's Furniture."

"Henry!" we both said in unison.

After we wolfed down lunch, we found Henry Mitchell and asked if he could get his dad to cut the board in his furniture shop.

"That looks scary," Henry said.

"Yeah," Max said. "It came from a wicked witch's house. Be careful with the nail."

"I use them every day in Dad's shop," Henry said. "It's not like I'm going to put it on the floor and step on it." He held up the board and prodded the rusty nail with his fingertip.

"Can you have it back tomorrow?" I asked and handed him a paper with the dimensions on it.

"It's only two cuts." Henry made two imaginary lines across the wood with his fingertip. "As long as the witch didn't cast some kind of spell on it and I cut my hand off or something, I should be able to do it tonight."

Max and I looked at each other. *The power of return*, I thought and wondered if he was thinking the same thing.

"You don't believe in all that stuff, do you, Henry?" Max asked.

Henry looked at Max, then at me. "Uh, I don't know. Why? Where did you get this?"

"It came out of our scrap pile at home," Max said. "It's from an old storage shed that fell down behind the house. We use the stuff in the winter for kindling. Just be careful."

Henry started swinging the board like some kind of primitive weapon as he walked down the hall.

I could tell English was going to be boring—again. How in the world could I ever learn all that stuff?

While we were supposed to be reading chapter seventeen, I reread the instructions I had printed out from the Internet. I figured as long as Henry cut the board to the dimensions on the paper I'd given him, it should fit my guitar. It looked like all I would have to do is wedge it in. I couldn't wait to try it. At least I would be able to audition. If I messed up, I could always blame the guitar.

The last bell rang, and I rushed to meet Henry at the buses to make sure he wouldn't forget to bring the board back the next day.

"Sorry," Henry said. "I don't have it."

"What do you mean? I've got to have it for an audition Saturday. Where is it?"

"You're going to audition with a piece of wood?"

"It's to fix my guitar with."

"Well, you remember the nail sticking out? When I went down the hall, Mr. Peterson saw me swinging the thing and confiscated it. I thought he was going to send me to Mrs. Fitzpatrick's office for having a weapon."

"Henry! We told you to be careful. Now what am I going to do?"

He laughed and pointed toward my bus. "You're going to miss your ride if you don't hurry. It's starting to move."

I hurtled toward the bus. Lightning shot up my whole arm when I slapped the glass on the door to get the driver to stop. The brace was good for keeping me from bending my finger, but it still hurt like crazy every time I bumped it.

The ride home gave me time to think. The only other person I knew with a guitar was one of my cousins in Knoxville, but I knew she wouldn't let me borrow hers.

There was no way I could ask Cory. I hoped

that when he found out what had happened, he would offer to loan me one. I couldn't refuse then.

When I got home, I called Max and told him the latest. "Maybe you should pray," he said. "I think the power of return is out to get you."

"Max, I'm serious."

"Well, one good thing is that your 'Unplugged' video count is still going up."

"How is that a good thing?"

"When you win the contest, you'll surprise everyone. Just think about the contrast. From 'Blues Fool' to 'Blues Star.'"

"I can't hold a pick. Even if I could, my guitar isn't worth playing. It won't stay in tune through a whole song. Especially if I bend a string. I'm doomed."

"Isn't there something else you can stick in the thing to block it up with?"

"Like what?"

"I don't know. Maybe something made of hard plastic or something."

"Duh, Einstein," I said. "What *kind* of something?"

"Eureka!" Max shouted. "That's it. I think I may have the perfect something for it. I'll be right over."

chapter THIRTEEN

"A BONE? YOU'VE GOT TO BE KIDDING, RIGHT? You want me to stick a dog bone in my guitar?"

"Just try it. It's about the right size, and besides, it's not really a bone. It's some kind of nylon or something. Einstein won't mind if you use it."

Of all the lamebrain ideas that Max came up with, sometimes they worked. We removed the back plate that covered the springs and stuff for the tremolo system, and I stuck the well-gnawed, blue bone down into the cavity where the instructions said to place a piece of wood. It was a perfect fit. The block holding the strings wouldn't budge. I almost bent the whammy bar checking to see if I could make it move.

"Wow!" I said.

He bowed and said, "*Bow*-wow, you mean. And now, here's Rodney Becker playing 'The Bow Wow Blues'! Maybe we can slice a piece off the end of the bone for you to use as a guitar pick. Then you can tell your guitar, 'I have a bone to pick *you* with.' You know, instead of I have a bone to pick with you. Get it?"

We laughed so hard I could hardly put the back plate on the guitar. After I got the new strings on, I still had a problem. I couldn't hold a pick.

"How about one of those thumb picks like banjo players use?" Max asked. "It just sticks on your thumb, doesn't it? You don't have to hold on to it, do you?"

"I don't know if I could. I wouldn't be able to play anything very fast. Besides, I don't have one."

"Maybe you can borrow one from Cory. He has a banjo. He must have a thumb pick."

"I guess I'll stick to finger picking. I'll just try not to use my bad one."

I plugged into my amp and cranked up the volume.

Bbzzzt rrrk. Bzzt. Bzzt bzzt rrrrrkkk!

"Now what?" Max asked.

I turned all the knobs on the guitar. Nothing but static. "It must have a short in the wiring." I turned down the amplifier, loosened the strings, and removed the knobs and pickguard from the guitar.

"Watch for spiders," Max said. There were cobwebs under the pickups. The wiring looked okay, but one wire was loose where the cord plugged into the jack.

"You know, I could wire in the MP3 player with your guitar song recorded on it and you could have a perfect audition."

"Would it fit in there?" I asked.

"I could remove a couple of those springs and put it back there. Then I could run wires to the output jack."

"How would I turn it on?"

"I'm not sure yet."

"Instead of lip-syncing, I'd be finger-syncing." Every time I held the loose wire, the guitar would sound normal.

"If I had known, I would have brought my soldering iron. If you want, we can take it to my house and fix it."

I kept thinking about the MP3 player idea all the way to Max's. As long as it was me playing on it, it wouldn't be cheating. Would it? After all, it was just an audition. All I had to do was show them I could play so I could be in the competition.

When we got to Cory's Tuesday evening, Myra had already started to record. As I watched, I imagined what it would be like if we were in a band together. I'd never felt anything like this for a girl before, but she was different. She played clarinet in school, and it was no big deal. But when she played the keyboard, I felt all weird inside.

Cory didn't say much. Like something was bothering him. I worried he knew what we had done and was waiting for the right moment to say something about it. Or maybe he was waiting to see if we would bring the bag back. Actually, it *was* back. I'd been carrying it in my pocket since that night in the graveyard.

I thought I might give it to him after we finished recording, but I figured if he didn't know about it, I would ruin everything. He'd probably kick us out and erase all my tracks.

"You okay, Cory?" I finally got up the nerve to ask after Myra finished.

"Yeah, just tired, I guess." His words came out

slowly. He rolled his chair back and stretched his arms in front of him, interlacing his fingers. When he turned his palms out, the popping reminded me of firecrackers it was so loud. "These ole bones are getting too old."

I pressed my hand on my pocket and felt the box inside the bag. *Not as old as these.*

Myra started playing some funky sounding reggae music on the keyboard. She had her eyes closed and rocked back and forth.

"If you two can come over next Monday night, we'll start mixing the tracks. I'll show you the ins and outs of the mixer. How's that sound?"

"Wow!" I said. "That sounds great."

"Yeah," Max said.

"Feedback, you can push the play button," Cory said.

Max held up his right index finger in front of his face and wiggled it. "I'll be ready."

We all laughed.

Cory pressed a mute button on the mixer. Myra's eyes opened wide. She sat motionless like something had scared her to death. "What was that?"

"Pure silence." Cory drew the words out and laughed. "Frightening, isn't it?"

"I thought I broke something," Myra answered. "Don't do that."

"It's a wrap," Cory said and clapped his hands. "We'll mix on Monday and maybe even burn a CD."

chapter
FOURTEEN

I COULDN'T BELIEVE HOW MANY GUITAR PLAYERS had shown up for the audition. *Eddie may be the least of my worries*, I thought. There were seventy-five other contestants to worry about on the list for my age group. A few of them went to Mountain Side Middle School, but I never knew they played guitar. Eddy and Kyle were already there. Eddie was showing off with his black Gibson SG, while Kyle was eating a sandwich.

"Look, they packed a lunch," Max said.

"Maybe we should have, too. It looks like we might be here a while."

The letter said to arrive at least thirty minutes before my audition time and that each contestant would have five minutes to perform. I decided to play the shortest song I knew. If I didn't get nervous and play too fast, I could make it last around two minutes. Cory said they always weed out the beginners who can't play and that I should do fine. Plus, I had the voodoo bag in my pocket. And my finger-syncing secret weapon for backup.

Some thin guy dressed in black and wearing a name tag that read *Lamon* paraded into the hall. "Can I have everyone's attention please?" He waited for everyone to be quiet, and I couldn't help thinking he looked like a character from a vampire movie with his pale skin and all. "Take one and pass them back." He handed a stack of papers to the girl at the front of the line. "This is the order you will be called, so pay attention. We have a lot of folks to hear today. If you are asked to stop playing, that means we've heard enough, so stop. Don't finish the song. If they ask you to stop, it doesn't mean you're not in. If you are to be in the main competition, you will receive an email by Wednesday. It will have all the information about the show day. Please be on time, or you will forfeit your slot. No exceptions. With all that said, have a great time." He pulled a remote control from his pocket, turned on a giant TV mounted on the wall, and left. The TV showed a view of the stage so we could watch each other's performances.

I ranked number forty-seven on the list.

"Wow, look at this." Max pointed to number forty-eight. Eddie. "At least you get to go on before him."

"I'm just worried about how good the other forty-six in front of me are," I said. "I may not have to worry about Eddie at all."

The first three guys were pretty good. None of them got to finish their song, though. The fourth one was pretty bad. He'd play a chord and then stick his right palm against the strings to mute them while he carefully repositioned his left hand into a new chord. I couldn't believe they let him play as long as they did. I wondered if they were making fun of him or something.

Number twenty-two was a plain-Jane looking girl with red hair and freckles. According to the list, her name was Victoria Valentine. I had seen her at school, but never paid much attention to her. She had some weird looking classical guitar, but I couldn't make out the brand. It looked like a rat had gnawed a hole through where the pickguard should have been.

Victoria climbed onto a stool, pushed up her

black-framed glasses, and started to play. At first, it sounded like some kind of lullaby, but after she got started, it was great. She was performing a piece called "Sunburst" by Andrew York. Her left hand was all over the place. It looked like a spider crawling up and down the guitar neck. She was incredible. No one in the theater made a sound. The judges let her play until the end of the song, and then the whole place burst into applause.

"I might as well just pack up and go," I told Max.

"She wasn't all that good," he said. Everyone around us stopped what they were doing and looked at him like he was an idiot. "I was just joking." Everyone laughed. Max looked at the floor and shook his head.

The air in the hall was getting warm. By the time they had called number thirty-five, I thought we were going to roast. Thirty-five looked like someone from a motorcycle gang with silver spikes sticking out of his belt, watchband, and guitar strap. He opened with some power chord, then backed up two steps, closed his eyes, and started shaking his head. "Oops," he said then took two steps forward and hit a different chord. He reminded me of me. The chord sounded good, but something had to be going wrong. He unplugged his guitar, started to cry, and ran off stage.

"Touchy," Max said. "Guess he's not as big, bad, and tough as he looks." Everybody laughed again.

I felt sorry for the guy. I knew how he felt. I'm glad I hadn't tried to look all tough and cool at the school talent show.

Lamon walked back out into the hall. "We are going to take a break. Go ahead and stretch your legs or take a restroom break. We'll sound a bell in ten minutes. When you hear it, be ready to continue.

After the break, the judges must have been getting tired because things moved fast. Either that, or I was getting nervous. When they called for number forty-five, we made our way toward the stage entrance. Eddy and Kyle were already there. Kyle was finishing another sandwich.

"Hey, it's Unplugged," Eddie said when we walked by. "Wow, what's that?" He reached for my guitar. "Can I see it?"

"Umm, I guess." Without thinking, I pulled the strap from my shoulder and offered the guitar to him. Max punched me in the side with his elbow. I wondered what Eddie might do to it. I imagined him messing with the tuning. Then I thought about him taking out a pair of wire cutters and cutting the strings off.

"It's a bummer your finger is still in that thing. Can you even play?" Eddie riffed a scale on my guitar.

"Yeah, it hurts, but I can," I said. Then he did something that really made me wonder what he was up to.

He offered his hand for me to shake and said, "Good luck out there."

From the way he was concerned with my finger, I was afraid he would squeeze it to make it start hurting. I put my right hand behind my back and offered him my other. He shook it with his left hand then went back to playing my guitar.

"Can I see yours?"

"Sure." He pointed to the SG. I figured if he did anything to mine, I could run with his. It was too close to my turn to have anything happen.

"Yeah, good luck on stage," Kyle said and offered me his left hand. We shook, and then I picked up the SG. When I tried to play a riff, I realized that Kyle's sandwiches had been peanut butter and jelly, which were all over his hand. Now the gooey mess was on my hand, and it was all over

Eddie's guitar neck. I put his guitar back into its case and asked Max for a hand wipe from my gig bag he was holding. I'd carried hand wipes and a towel with my guitar ever since that first night at Cory's.

"Getting nervous?" Eddie asked.

"Yeah, sweaty palms I guess." I wiped the goo from my hands.

"Number forty-seven."

"You're up," Max said.

Eddie handed me my guitar, but as I was putting the strap over my head, my splint got tangled in it. It felt like my finger was being ripped off. As I walked out, Lamon handed me a guitar cord. I plugged it in and had a flashback to the day in the gymnasium. My finger ached, but I had to try. I closed my eyes and bowed my head, took a deep breath, and played. Their sound system rocked. They even had a bit of chorus effect on my amp like I had asked for in the special information field on the sign-up sheet. I bumped the splint on the high E string once, and it made a buzzing sound, but all the other notes were clear. I looked up. The place was full. I guess it was family of the other kids along with the adult competitors. I felt a peaceful cool breeze blowing on me. Sort of like the one in the graveyard before the monsoon.

"Thank you, Rodney, that will be enough," one of the judges said.

"Thank you," I said. As I walked off stage, pulling the guitar strap over my head, something yanked the guitar out of my hands. It plummeted to the stage floor with a clang. I'd been so busy not being nervous that I forgot to unplug the cord. My cool breeze morphed into a heat wave like that day in the gymnasium. I felt my face turning its new natural shade.

I was picking up the guitar when Lamon rushed over to me. The bump on the ground must have turned on the MP3 player because my song started to play. I strummed my fingers across the strings extra hard to cover its sound and jerked the cord out of the guitar. It had only played four notes. I hoped no one else had noticed. I had made it through the whole audition playing for real. Now all I needed was to be disqualified for cheating.

"Sorry," I said.

"Your guitar okay?" Lamon asked.

"I guess. It's already messed up, so it couldn't have hurt it much." When I picked up the guitar, I heard something rattling inside. I figured it was trashed.

"Number forty-eight," a judge's voice blared over the sound system.

Max came running to meet me. "You were great! Except when you forgot to unplug."

We were almost to the front door when we heard Eddie. He played one note, stopped, and yelled for Kyle to bring out his guitar case.

One of the judges reminded him that he had only five minutes to play.

I turned to see what was happening. Eddie was wiping his left hand on his jeans. The stage microphone must have been extra sensitive because even from where we were, we could hear Eddie mumbling something about peanut butter and jelly.

chapter
FIFTEEN

It was 2:08 when I got home. Mom had left a note saying that someone called in sick and she had to go to work early. For lunch, I decided to try my luck with leftovers. I found a piece of pizza and part of a chocolate cake.

Max had to go do family stuff. If you call clothes shopping at the mall in Knoxville *family stuff*. That left me with me. I had the whole afternoon to myself to figure out what was wrong with my guitar. Afraid of what I might find, I took off the back plate. I was scared the MP3 player had come loose and messed up the wiring again, but it was still stuck tight with the duct tape Max had used on it. The problem was Einstein's bone. It must have jarred loose when the guitar fell. After I wedged it back in, it worked great. I got the guitar back in tune and plugged it into the amp. It was fine. For once since we'd done the voodoo spell, something worked right.

I thought about everything that had gone wrong and wondered if the power of return was finished. At least three bad things had already happened. Some of it rubbed off on Eddie in the form of gooey peanut butter and jelly. Guess it really is bad luck to shake a left hand.

I couldn't stop thinking about all the hoodoo, voodoo, and witch's spells Max put in his folder. I needed to give them back but didn't know if I might need them again for something. No red-blooded American teen should be without his or her own book of spells.

Maybe I could make copies and sell them to all the kids at school. Maybe give some free samples to the kids who needed the most help, like Benji Springer. He needed all the help he could get with everything. Maybe he could find a spell and get back at all the people who bullied him. I thought I could make hundreds or maybe thousands of dollars. I could even sell them on an *as-needed* basis.

Ring. Ring.

Wow, my first customer, I imagined. The thought gave me goose bumps.

"Hello?"

"Rodney? It's Myra."

"Uh," I said. "Yeah, it's me. How's it going? I mean—"

"I'm spending the night with Uncle Cory. He's taking me out for pizza and to the movies. He said I could see if you might want to go with us to celebrate your audition."

"Sure, I guess." I wondered how he knew the audition went okay. Had he been there? I felt something stir in my stomach again. "What time?"

"We'll be heading out around five. We can pick you up if you'll be ready."

"Sure."

I couldn't believe it. Twice in one day something good had happened. Who would have ever thought Myra would ask me out? Or any girl for that matter? I felt like my luck was taking a turn for the better.

Cory took us to Pizza Plaza. We had double cheese with pepperoni and pineapple. Cory was fun for an old man. I wondered if he was trying to set up Myra and me since he'd seen me staring at her in the recording studio. It didn't matter if it was Cory or the voodoo. Whatever it was, it was cool.

The theater was packed even though the movie wasn't all that great. Part five of some zombie-love movie. Kind of a chick flick, but there were a lot of guys there. Guess watching chick flicks is the price guys pay for having a date.

The three of us shared a large bucket of popcorn. Myra held it on her lap between Cory and me. Sometimes, when things got tense on the screen, Myra would rest her wrist on the side of the bucket with her hand down in the popcorn. When I would reach for some, our hands would touch. We started some kind of game by rubbing the oily popcorn butter all over each other's hands. I stopped when I smeared butter on Cory's hand by mistake and he slapped at me.

Cory leaned across Myra and whispered, "You're going to lose another finger if you keep that up."

I thought Myra was going to die from laughing so hard. I knew my face was red, but it didn't bother me. Maybe because we were in the dark. I tried to hold it in, but Myra kept laughing, and I busted up.

Everyone started shushing us. That just made it worse. I had to go to the lobby because I was laughing so hard.

By the time I had composed myself and made it back to my seat, the movie was almost over. I don't remember much about what happened on the screen, but it was the best movie I had ever been to. At least until the three of us walked into the lobby.

I had crammed the napkin I wiped all the butter on from my hand into my left jeans pocket. When I pulled it out, Cory's voodoo bag fell to the floor. I froze. I looked at him. If Cory saw it, and I don't know how he could have kept from seeing it, he didn't let on. Finally able to move, I picked it up.

"I guess it's time to call it a night." Cory pulled his car keys from his pocket and twirled them on his index finger the way gunslingers used to do with their pistols in those old TV westerns.

"Yeah," I said. "I guess so."

He saw it. He had to see it. He couldn't help but see it. The thoughts kept going through my head. I figured my luck had run out.

chapter
SIXTEEN

"You're grounded!" Mom informed me when I walked through the door. She was sitting on the couch in the dark. "Where on earth have you been?" She switched on the lamp.

"I went to the movies with Cory and Myra. It's just ten-thirty."

"It would have been decent of you to have called me before you left. Or at least left a note. All I got was pizza bones on the table and a to-go box. Max didn't even know where you were. That's a first. As far as I knew, you could have been dead somewhere."

"Then you would be free. Just like Dad." It came out louder than I meant for it to.

Mom was silent. Her lips tightened, and her

eyes narrowed. The world stopped. I was scared to move.

She had enough time to yell, but she didn't.

"I'm fine," I said.

Mom still didn't say anything.

"We just went to Pizza Plaza and then to the movies." I was far from dead. I'd been having the time of my life.

"Then you drove right by the diner. You could have at least stopped in and told me. We serve pizza. Remember?"

"Mom, I just didn't think about it."

"You're just like your dad. He didn't think about telling me things either. You two deserve each other."

"Oh, so you *do* want me to go with him?"

"Rodney! That's enough. You're grounded." She sprang up and turned toward the kitchen.

"From what?"

"Life. Everything. There'll be no Cory. No movies. No pizza. No nothing for two weeks."

"Mom, I have to play in the competition."

She turned, crossed her arms, and squinted. "Rodney, you don't *have* to do anything but go to school and come home. I don't want to hear any more about it."

I ran to my room and slammed the door. Blue lights flashed through my side window. When Mom freaked out, she went all the way. She must have called Jeff to report a missing child. I wondered which photo she gave them to use in the Amber Alert.

I stepped into the hallway and yelled, "I'm not a baby."

I heard her tell Jeff that I was home and everything was okay. A few minutes later, the blue lights stopped, and the car pulled away.

I guess it was good that Mom had someone to turn to when she needed something. Jeff wasn't bad, but he made me nervous, him being a cop and all.

I pulled Max's voodoo folder out of the closet to find something to help me get ungrounded. I had to go to the competition. Even if it meant using some kind of spell on Mom. I found one I thought might work that called for some weird stuff I had never heard of. Stuff like Angelica root and Gilead buds. I'd also need to come up with flax seeds, rose oil, lavender flowers, basil leaves, and a metal dove-with-olive-branch charm. I was supposed to put it all, along with a note with Mom's name and mine on it, into a pale blue flannel bag. This was supposed to bring harmony into the home. It had to be worth a try. I had nothing left to lose. If nothing else, it would make a great air freshener. At least it didn't say anything about a graveyard.

I pulled Cory's bag out of my pocket and sniffed it. It smelled like someone had wiped their sweaty underarm with it after they'd played basketball for six hours. I wondered what made it all work. I looked at the poster and thought a simple rabbit's foot would have been easier, but I didn't know where to get one. I sure couldn't go out and catch a rabbit and cut its foot off. Occasionally, I would see one that had been run over in the road. Not that I could imagine myself bringing home roadkill and sawing off its foot. We didn't even have a saw. I would have had to take it to Henry at school and get him to cut it off in his dad's shop.

I wondered if the spell with the pink birthday candle had anything to do with Myra asking me out. The movie thing could have been Cory's idea, or maybe Myra was just being nice.

Before I went to bed, I checked the "Unplugged" count. It was at 8,549. There were comments from some girls saying stuff like "Aw, poor guy." Some of the ones from the guys were pretty bad. I guess I was getting used to it, because I was kind of proud the count had gotten so high. I wondered if I would be asked to be on a TV show for getting so many hits. I might become a star after all. I thought I would get Max to record me at the Music Today competition, and if I did okay, he could upload it as the sequel to "Unplugged." I would call it "Plugged In."

In bed, I wondered if there were any spells I could use to make my finger better. The more I thought about everything, the more I worried what might happen if it messed up. My finger was already hurt. I couldn't imagine having the power of return coming back on it.

chapter SEVENTEEN

I THOUGHT MOM WOULD PUT UP A FIGHT WHEN I told her I didn't want to go to church Sunday morning, but she didn't. She'd grounded me, so that meant I couldn't go anywhere, and church was about the last thing on my mind.

When Mom left, I looked up all the stuff for her spell on the Internet. Angelica root was some kind of parsley. Gilead buds were a kind of organic aspirin from a poplar tree. I found basil leaves and dried parsley in Mom's spice rack. The medicine cabinet had aspirin and a bottle of flax seed oil capsules. Mom had some lavender bubble bath, but I would have to get the rose oil from Max.

I took one of my old blue flannel shirts and cut around the pocket. I figured it was as close to a pouch as I could make without having to sew anything. I didn't know where Mom would keep a needle and thread, or if we even had them. I went through her jewelry box but didn't find any charms of a dove with an olive branch. I did find a paper-thin brass bookmarker that had some kind of bird holding an arrow in its beak. It was too long, so I bent it double to make it fit in the pocket. It would have to do.

I ripped off a corner of notebook paper and wrote our names—Sarah and Rodney—then folded it. Before I stuffed it in with everything else, I opened it up and wrote Dad's name on it, too.

By the time Mom got home, I had gathered everything except the rose oil. She didn't say much. She just came in and started her daily cleaning routine. I went to my room and called Max.

"I need some of your rose oil," I said. "I'm going to try to fix Mom."

"You doing another spell?"

"Yeah, I found one. Says it's for harmony at home. I'm grounded, but I have to get her to let me go to Cory's and to the competition."

"Why don't you just sneak out?"

"If it works, the spell will be a lot easier."

"Yeah, and if it doesn't, you'll be grounded for the rest of your life. Or three lifetimes."

"Can you just bring the rose oil to school tomorrow? I don't even know if I'll get to go to Cory's."

"Sure. See ya tomorrow."

I finished putting all the stuff into the pocket, then tied an old leather boot string around its top. It looked cool. It made me think of a voodoo bag for a lumberjack because of the pattern of the material. The lavender bath oil made it smell like something a girl would carry. I only put a couple drops on the cloth, but it was strong. It did smell a lot better than Cory's voodoo bag, though.

"Rodney?" Mom called. "You want to go to town with me?"

"No," I yelled back. I stuffed the voodoo bag in my backpack and went to the bathroom to wash the smell off my hands.

"You been taking a bubble bath in there?" Mom asked when I walked into the living room. "You smell fresh as a flower."

"No, I kinda spilled your bath stuff. I guess all the smell didn't come off. Mom, can I go to Cory's tomorrow?" I thought the new voodoo bag might be working already.

"Rodney, I told you you're grounded."

I thought wrong. "But Cory is supposed to mix down my CD. It's what we've been working on all this time."

"I don't want to hear any more about it. And you better not leave this house while I'm gone."

"Will you just think about it? I promise I won't ever leave without telling you again. Think about it. Okay?"

"Good-bye, Rodney."

Maybe I should have gone with her to butter her up.

chapter EIGHTEEN

"YOU GOING BACK TO THE GRAVEYARD?" MAX asked.

"No, I don't have to for this one."

"You gonna eat your roll?

"Yeah, why?"

"What do you mean? You never eat your roll. You always give it to me."

I threw the roll to him. It bounced off his milk carton and landed in his peas.

"Well, if it isn't Smooth Move Rodney and Max-electro." Eddie slapped the table beside Max. "Nice audition the other day. I don't know what you did, but I know there's no way you could play like that with your finger messed up. You got a wireless receiver put in your guitar with someone else playing somewhere?" He tried to look cool tossing up an apple and catching it with the same hand.

"You're crazy. It was me playing."

"It's funny how your guitar started playing by itself when you dropped it on stage. There were so many other people warming up in there, no one would have noticed if someone else was playing and transmitting it to your guitar."

"I think you need to get your ears checked," I said.

"I think we should get your guitar checked to see what you've got rigged up inside it."

Max joined in with, "Hey, Eddie, I think we need to check your head and see what you've got rigged up inside there. We know it's not a brain."

"Hey, Rodney, catch." Eddie tossed the apple toward my right side. I guess he knew my reflexes would take over and I would try to catch it with my right hand. He was right. I tried to catch the apple. The one thing he didn't think about was what my reflexes would cause me to do when I caught it and it hit my splint.

I was never into sports because I couldn't throw a ball straight, but if there had been a scout watching at that moment, I might have changed my dream of being a musician.

Pain from my finger shot up my arm, and I threw the apple with more force than I ever knew existed in me. It hit Eddie's nose and bounced onto Max's plate. Blood splattered everywhere. Eddie grabbed his nose with both hands as the blood oozed down his face and dripped onto his shirt.

"You're dead, Becker. You just wait. They're going to hear about your electronically rigged guitar at the competition, too. You're going down."

"Oh, man, Eddie. I'm sorr—"

Max kicked my leg under the table and mouthed the words, "Don't apologize."

I continued with, "I'm sure they'll believe you. What proof do you have?"

"You just wait," he said and turned.

Eddie looked like some kind of bird swallowing a fish as he walked away with his nose pointed straight up. Guess he didn't know he'd have to swallow all the blood that way. I hoped it took him a long time to get the bleeding to stop.

I wiped Eddie's spattered blood off my arm with a paper napkin and held it up. "Think we can use this in a spell?"

"That's gross," Max said. "You got him good, though. Look at the apple. It's got his nose imprint on it." Max held the apple by its stem at arm's length like it was a dead rat. "What a waste." He let the apple drop onto the table beside him. The way the light reflected off the nose dent made it look like the skull from a shrunken head. I wondered if Max's Baphomet folder had anything about shrinking heads.

"Did you bring the rose oil?" I asked.

"Yeah. Where's the voodoo bag?"

"In my locker."

When we got there, we were greeted with "Air guitar champion and cheater!" printed on a piece of fluorescent orange card stock. It also had the web address to my "Unplugged" video. I ripped it off and let it fall to the floor. The aroma of lavender wafted from the vents as I worked the combination lock.

"You're going to mix rose oil with that? You should have put it in one of those resealable zipper bags so it doesn't smell so much."

I dripped three drops of rose oil into the bag and retied the leather shoestring around the top. The smell was strong—so strong you could probably smell it all throughout the school.

"I don't know if it will work on your mom, but I bet it would get you a date for the eighth-grade prom. Want me to bring you one of my mom's lipsticks?"

I slammed the locker door, shoved the aromatic voodoo bag against Max's shirt, and rubbed.

"Hi-ya-ha." Max gave some weird kung fu chop to my wrist, knocking the bag out of my hand. It flew about ten feet then slid another five on the floor. It stopped in front of the boys' restroom door. When Kyle Reed stepped out of the restroom, he gave the bag a kick that bounced it off the opposite wall. When he saw Max and me running toward it, he lurched across the hall and grabbed it.

"You looking for this?" Kyle scrunched up his nose at the smell of the bag. "What is it? You guys collecting urinal deodorant in your little sachet bag?"

"You mean those things you use for breath mints that you get from the boys' room?" I said.

"Hi-ya-ha!" Max let out another kung fu yell and gave Kyle's arm one of his Karate chops. The bag went flying again. It flew almost straight up. I grabbed for it just as Kyle was stepping toward me. The end of my aluminum splint hit Kyle in the nose. Right between both nostrils. Lightning shot from my finger all the way to my elbow.

"Aaiiigh!" I yelled.

"What's going on out here?" Mrs. Fitzpatrick popped out of the girls' bathroom.

"Just goofing around," Max said.

"Then why is his nose bleeding?"

"He ran into Rodney's finger," Max tried to explain. "Well, he fell into it. Sort of."

"All three of you, to my office. Now!"

chapter
NINETEEN

MAX'S ZIPPER BAG IDEA WORKED. I PUT THE
voodoo bag in one and shoved it between Mom's
mattress and box spring. I couldn't smell anything,
but I wondered if it was because I had smelled it all
day and was used to it.

There was no way I was going to ask Mom to
sign the note from Mrs. Fitzpatrick before I got
back from Cory's. If she found out I'd been in the
principal's office, she would have grounded me for
another month.

Mrs. Fitzpatrick had let Kyle, Max, and me off
with a warning. I had never gotten one before. She
told me if I got two more, it would mean a three-
day suspension. If Kyle hadn't agreed that it was an
accident, we would have been suspended for

fighting. I guess he didn't want to admit that I gave him a bloody nose in a fight. Being in an accident sounded better for his ego, but the rumors going around the school made me out to be some kind of Golden Glove champion. I had never been in a fight before. Much less given anyone a bloody nose —much less two in one day.

"Mom," I said when I walked into the kitchen. She was pulling a to-go box out of the microwave. "Did you think more about letting me go to Cory's tonight so I can get a copy of my CD?"

"You better be home by nine-thirty. Not one minute later."

"You wouldn't drive me, would you?"

"You ride that bike everywhere. Now you want me to be your personal taxi?"

"I just thought if you picked me up, I couldn't be late. If I am, it's your fault."

She glared at me. "Just be home before nine-thirty."

"Thanks, Mom," I yelled on my way out.

Cory asked Max and me to wait in the moat room. "I have a potential client. You guys may know him."

Of all the people in the world who could have been sitting in the control room, it was Eddie.

"You going to do a CD for him?" I asked.

"Well, he said it depended on his parents. He's going to hit them up for the money."

The fact that Cory was going to charge Eddie didn't outweigh the fact that Eddie and Myra looked like they were having a good time all alone in the little room. I couldn't hear what they were saying, but Eddie kept looking my way and nodding his head at me. Then they would laugh. His nose still looked bruised. I wondered if he told Myra about the apple incident.

"Hang tight," Cory said. "We'll be finished in a bit." Cory walked into the control room and sat beside Myra.

"Hey, look," Max said. He handed me a brochure from the Les Paul table. It was about Cory's recording studio, listing all the features and rates.

"Wow," I said. "I hope he doesn't decide to charge me. I'd owe him a fortune."

"Or your soul," Max added. He pointed to a line on the brochure. "What's a hundred dollars an hour—with a two-hour minimum, of course—to a school kid who makes ten dollars a week mowing a yard?"

"Look at this," I said. "We could book a whole day for only six hundred and fifty dollars."

"Why not just buy the studio and hire Cory to run it for you?"

Cory opened the control room door and stepped out in front of Eddie. "Give me a call when you're ready, and I'll fix you up."

"Okay," Eddie said. "I'll let you know something in a day or two. Oh yeah, Myra"—Eddie turned back to her—"I may take you up on your offer for some keyboard parts." As he turned toward the stairs, he narrowed his eyes at me and paused like he wanted to speak. Before he could say anything, his cell phone rang. He poked his pointer finger toward me and mouthed, "Cheater," then continued to the staircase. "Yes, Mom. I know. I'm on my way out right now." Cory followed Eddie upstairs.

"Hey, Rodney," Myra said. "How's the finger?"

"It's getting there," I said. "You doing keyboards for Eddie now?"

"I might. If he hires me."

"Are you going to send Rodney a bill?" Max asked.

"Hmm," Myra said and smiled. "Maybe I'll let him owe me. He'll never know when I'm going to collect."

"Hello, boys," Cory said, coming down the stairs. "You ready to mix?"

"Sure," I said.

"Absolutely," Max added.

We followed Cory into the control room and took our places. "No headphones for mixdown," he said. "They lie. I'm going to put your ears to the test."

"Which is better, sound A or sound B?" Cory pushed buttons and slid sliders. It was like going to the eye doctor. I think he knew what each one needed, but was letting us see, or hear, the process of mixing. I couldn't hear the difference between some of the settings. I guess his ears were trained for stuff that regular people couldn't hear.

When we finished, Cory handed me a CD. "Here you go. Hope this is payment enough for helping me work the bugs out of the system. It's hard to do if I'm recording myself, and I hate trying to do it when I'm working with paying customers. They tend to see dollar signs with every tick of the clock and start to get nervous when I'm experimenting and playing around. Besides, most adults are know-it-alls. They try to tell *me* what to do. You were great. You played and let me work."

He looked at Max and handed him a CD also. "Feedback, I'm going to make an audio engineer out of you yet."

"Wow," I said. "Thanks. This is great. I have a real CD."

"Well, son," Cory added, "it's master quality. It's good enough to replicate and sell. Now I'm talking about the quality of the recording. The song you wrote and your playing are good, but it's up to your fans to decide if they are willing to pay for it."

"You mean I could sell this?" I asked.

"Well," Cory stretched out the word. "You could, but remember that it's just one song. You'd need to tell everyone it's a single sample, not a full CD. Maybe you can save some money and record more songs to make a full CD. Of course, I might be persuaded to give you a discount on studio time since you're Myra's friend."

We all laughed. "So I can make copies on my computer?" I asked.

"Yeah, you could, or I have a duplicator. I can run them in batches of up to twenty at a time. Of course, I would have to charge for the blank CDs, though."

I had lost all track of time. I looked at my watch. It was 9:20. "I've got to go, or I'll be late."

"Hey, Cinderella, it's still a few hours 'til midnight," Max said.

"It'll be worse than turning into a pumpkin. I'll be grounded for life. See you all."

chapter
TWENTY

MOM MUST HAVE REALLY LOST IT. OF ALL THE lame things to do, she sent Jeff, blue lights and all. According to my watch, I still had five minutes to get home.

"Rodney, get in," Jeff's voice blared through his car's loudspeaker.

I couldn't believe I was being arrested for being late. I wondered what Mom would do if she knew we had taken Cory's voodoo bag. Send me to prison? Maybe she found the note from Mrs. Fitzpatrick.

"What about my bike?" I yelled.

"Ditch it. I'll come back for it later. It's your mom. She's in the hospital. Get in."

"What happened?" I shouted. I threw the

bicycle in the ditch and climbed into the cruiser.

"She had a fall. She hit her head and has a broken arm."

I just sat and listened. If I hadn't been so worried about Mom, the ride to the hospital would have been cool. The strobe effect of the blue lights made everything look weird after a while. We were there in about ten minutes.

When we walked into Mom's room, she had her eyes closed. Was she dead? "Mom?" I whispered. "You awake?"

"Rodney?" Mom's voice cracked when she tried to speak. "Yeah, I'm awake. Come on in." Mom rose up and tried to adjust her pillow.

"You okay?" I fixed her pillow and pressed the button to raise the bed so she could sit up. She looked helpless. I had never seen her that way. There was a tube coming out of her good arm, and her left one had a cast from her wrist to her underarm. The doctors had wrapped gauze around the top of her head.

"I was trying to clean that stupid ceiling fan over my bed. I got too close to the edge and down I went. I turned to catch myself but landed on my arm and hit my head on the corner of the chest of drawers."

My mouth dropped open. The chest was at the corner of the bed where I'd put her voodoo bag.

"Rodney? You okay?" Mom asked.

"Uh, yeah." I couldn't believe I had almost killed my mom. First my finger, then my guitar, now my mom. "Just worried, I guess. How long do you have to stay here?"

"The doctor wants to keep an eye on me overnight. Jeff can take you to his place, or you can go home."

"Home's fine. Unless you want me to stay here with you."

"No, you need your rest. Just go on home, but let Ms. Lane know that you're there alone. She'll keep an eye on you."

Jeff gave me a ride and made me promise to call his cell if I needed anything. I promised, even though I couldn't think of any reason I would need to call. I'd rather call 911 and get a potluck cop if anything happened. If Jeff was in the middle of a shootout somewhere, I would have to wait until it was over before he could get to me.

The house was dark, warm, and quiet when I went in. I called Ms. Lane, then double-checked the door locks like Mom told me, and went to bed.

Rat-a-tat. Rat-a-tat.

The tapping sound came from the direction of my desk where I had put the bag with the finger bones.

Rat-a-tat. Rat-a-tat.

I thought of Edgar Allan Poe's poem about the raven tapping on his window. I turned on my bedside lamp.

Rat-a-tat.

"This is crazy," I said out loud. I picked up the phone, in case I needed to call Jeff or 911, then got up and turned on the overhead light. The air in the room suddenly felt like someone had turned on the air conditioner.

I thought it could be my guilty conscience like the guy in Poe's "The Tell-Tale Heart."

"Dead fingers don't tap," I told myself. It had to be all in my mind. I must have been feeling guilty for having Cory's dead fingers. I wondered if I would go crazy like the guy in the story. Just my luck —The Tell-Tale Fingers.

If I wasn't going crazy, then the fingers were really tapping. I finally got the courage to take a step toward my desk.

Nothing.

Another step.

Nothing still.

I inched closer and stared at the bag. I reached out and gently ran my finger across the soft black leather.

Rat-a-tat.

That's when I died.

At least, that was probably what it sounded like from my scream.

After the screaming stopped, rigor mortis struck again when I saw a shadow on the window behind my desk. It looked like an old man's deformed finger pointing at me.

Rat-a-tat.

Outside, the tip of a limb from the old oak tree behind the house was hitting the window when the wind blew. I stuffed the bag under the blanket with the folder in the closet.

I figured the safest place to sleep was on the couch in the living room, away from the voodoo bag and Baphomet. I could still hear the wind blowing stuff around outside, so I turned on the radio to cover the sounds. That was at 1:32 a.m.

chapter TWENTY-ONE

WHEN I WOKE UP, THE PAIN IN MY FINGER WAS gone. I wondered if it was because I had put the voodoo bag under the blanket in my closet. Maybe it was acting like a blanket of protection. Then I realized I couldn't feel my hand either. I pulled my arm from under my granny's homemade throw pillow I had slept on to see if my hand was even still there. It was, but it was numb. When the phone rang, I knocked the table lamp to the floor trying to answer it.

"Rodney? What was that?"

"Nothing, Mom. I dropped something. How are you feeling?" When I tried to pick up the lamp, the feeling of needles started in my hand. The lamp fell again.

"I just wanted to check on you before you went to school. Did everything go all right?"

"Yeah, I'm fine."

"Do you need Jeff to come by or anything?"

"No, but could you ask him to bring my bike home? I need to go to Cory's when I get out of school."

I finally got my rubber hand to work enough to get the lamp back on the table.

"Do you think you'll be getting out today?" I noticed the clock. I had ten minutes to catch the bus.

"I hope so. They said they want to run some more tests. If they want to keep me too long, I may have to call your dad to see if he can come stay with you until I get out."

"Mom, I'm fine by myself. I don't need him. I've got Ms. Lane. Besides, you can have Jeff stop by and check on me." *Anything but Dad.* "Hey, it's almost time for the bus. I gotta go."

"Love you."

"Love you, too."

I ran to my room, grabbed Cory's bag and Baphomet, then stuffed them into my backpack. In Mom's room, I took the voodoo bag from under the mattress and tossed it in, too. I felt like a walking occult store. *Need a spell? Got voodoo? I do. Hoodoo? That, too. Just call Rodney. A spell for every occasion. Never mind the fine print. The oh-so-small chance that the power of return will get you. No worries. If you're down enough to need a voodoo spell, what's a little bad luck? If you're gonna play the game, you gotta pay the price.*

The bus was just arriving when I got to the stop.

I waited at Max's homeroom. When he walked in, I shoved the Baphomet folder flat against his chest.

"What's this?" he asked.

"Your stupid spells. We've got to reverse them."

"What's going on?"

"I almost killed Mom." I kept shoving him until we were back in the hallway. He held the folder against his chest with his folded arms. "That power of return thing is getting out of hand."

"What happened to your mom? Is she okay?"

"She's in the hospital. She has a broken arm and maybe a concussion."

"Well, what do you want *me* to do?"

"You've got to meet me at Cory's tonight to give

his voodoo bag back." I held my splinted finger up in front of him. "It's probably why this thing isn't getting better."

"If you'd quit trying to catch things with it or using it to hit people in the nose, it might have a chance."

"This ain't a game anymore." I slapped the folder with my open palm. Max's eyes widened as he stumbled backward. "Just be there tonight."

When I got home, I called Mom's room at the hospital. A nurse told me they had taken her for more tests. My bicycle wasn't home yet, so the only way I could get to Cory's was to walk. I shoved Cory's voodoo bag into my pocket and put Mom's in a plastic grocery bag and took off.

I had been about halfway home when Jeff told me to put my bicycle in the ditch. I hoped he hadn't already picked it up. If he had, I would have to walk all the way. The more I thought about it, the faster I walked. The rain started just as I reached the spot where I had stashed the bike.

I stood there in the downpour, staring at

crumpled grass and weeds where the bike had been. It was about the same distance to my house or to Cory's.

I turned toward Cory's.

chapter
TWENTY-TWO

"You're soaked, son," Cory said. "Get on in here."

"Is Max here?" I stepped in and looked around. "He's supposed to meet me."

"No. Haven't seen him. Stay right there. I'll grab a towel."

Cory went down a hallway. Across the room was the stand where Max had put the fake voodoo bag. If I hadn't been soaked, I could have sneaked over and put the real one back. The way water was dripping off me, there was no way I could have dried the floor before Cory returned.

"Here," Cory said and tossed me a blue and orange, extra fluffy beach towel. "Now, what's up?"

I wasn't sure where to begin. I dried off the best I could.

"I..." I guess I freaked out because telling him we took his voodoo bag came out as, "I was wondering if you can mix me a CD of just my backing tracks for the competition. I'll pay for it."

"I'm sure I can." Cory walked to the stairs that led to the recording studio and motioned for me to follow. "I've saved all the settings on the automation track. All I have to do is mute your guitar track and it will mix itself. It'll sound just like the CD."

"That'll be great."

"We call them Flying Faders," Cory said when he saw me watching the controllers on the mixing board move by themselves. "The automation track remembers all the settings from when I recorded the master mix."

We listened to the CD, and when he started printing a label, I told him I needed to use the bathroom. I figured I was dry enough by then. I hurried up the stairs and to the little glass case where the fake voodoo bag was. I made the switch then ran to flush the commode. I didn't think Cory could hear, but I wanted to be safe. He was putting the CD in a case when I walked back in.

"Thanks. It sounded great," I said. "Now I

don't have to use those lame karaoke tracks anymore."

"It'll sound better when you're on stage playing along with it." He held up the CD and said, "Now, how about telling me what's really going on? I *know* you didn't come out in that downpour just to get a CD."

"It's Mom. She's in the hospital." My throat felt weird. I couldn't swallow. "She fell off the bed where I had put a voodoo bag."

Cory's eyes widened. "Voodoo bag? You mean, like, a mojo bag?"

"A voodoo bag, like yours." I took Mom's voodoo bag out of the grocery bag and offered it to him. He held his hands up, palms out, and leaned back in his chair. "Something went wrong. The power of return about killed Mom. It's the reason I almost broke my finger. And why Dad took my guitar. You've got to help."

"Slow down a little. Back up and tell me what's going on."

I explained the stuff we had found on the Internet about him selling his soul and the finger bones and how we used voodoo bags to do the spells. I just didn't tell him we had used his.

"And you believe all the junk you read on the Internet?"

He swiveled his chair around and shut down the recording equipment.

"It's not all lies. I did lose everything. My family, my house, and my music career because of two stupid habits. I used to drink, and I used to gamble. When I did both, things got bad. One night, a bunch of friends and I were playing a game of dice. I'd been drinking quite a bit. Actually, more than quite a bit. I was so drunk I didn't know what I was doing. They told me I was on a winning streak. Wiping them all out."

Cory went to a file cabinet and took a photo album from it. "Take a look." He opened it and pointed to a photo of a man standing with a woman wearing a wedding dress in front of a large two-story house.

"They tell me I said, 'I can't lose, and I want it all. I'll bet you this beautiful home you gentlemen are sitting in against whatever cash you have on you right now.' They all were decent enough not to take advantage of a drunk. All of them except Dr. Jesse Sketcher. He took me up on the bet. Of all the bets I had won that night, that one roll of the dice cost me everything. That's about the time I passed out.

"The next morning, Dr. Sketcher called to say he would meet me down at the courthouse so I could sign the papers over to him. He gave me a receipt and the two dice we had been rolling the night before.

"When my wife, Jenny, found out what I'd done, she packed up Tamara's diaper bag and they left. Haven't heard from her since. Well, she did send me divorce papers. And her wedding ring because it had been my grandmother's."

He turned the page in the album. "This is her just a few days before they left."

It was a black and white photo of a girl sitting on the hood of a white car and holding a baby. The car had a ribbon around it with a bow on the top. She looked peaceful, her head tilted to her left, and she was smiling. A faint smile washed across Cory's face and he rubbed the silver band on his ring finger. He sat motionless and silent—staring at the photo. After a couple of minutes, his smile faded.

Cory's voice cracked as it broke the silence. "Now as far as the little bag goes"—he cleared his throat—"that's where things got twisted around. When I lost the house, and my Jenny left, I hit the bottle real hard." He flipped through the pages until he came to a photo of a graveyard. "One night, I felt like I was ready to just give up and die. I got me a bottle, that little bag you read about, and I went to visit an old friend. Ole Joe. Joe Mullins was his name, but we used to call him Blues Mullins. He's the one who pretty much taught me everything I know about a guitar. He was my hero. I would have to say he's the best blues player who ever lived. He drank himself to death.

"I was feeling bad and needed a friend so I went up to his grave and drank about half the bottle. I'll never forget how he used to say, 'Gimme dat. Gimme dat bottle. I'll show you how to drink it.' Then he would give a big toothless grin, slurp some whiskey down, and play the blues."

Cory tapped his finger on one of the graves in the picture.

"I sat on his grave and dumped the rest of the bottle on him. I thought I heard him saying, 'Gimme dat.' That's the last drink I ever took. I dug a hole right on top of his grave to bury the dice Dr. Sketcher had given me. I was going to put our wedding rings in there, too. After I dug the hole, I just sat and stared into it. I wanted to bury my past along with the dice and our wedding rings. The more I stared at the hole, the more I thought about what I was about to do.

"I realized that sticking all that stuff in a hole wasn't going to get rid of my blues. I decided I should keep the dice to remind me of all I had lost. I called them my blues bones because they were made from bone. I shoved the dirt back in the hole and told Joe what I had done. When he was finished listening, I stuffed the dice and our wedding rings into a matchbox that I carried one of Ole Joe's guitar picks in for good luck. Guess that's when I started my collection of picks. I put the box back into the leather pouch he had given me. When the tears stopped, I stumbled toward town."

Cory flipped through more pages and stopped on a publicity photo of him holding a guitar. In the picture, he was smiling and pointing to a small bag hanging from the neck of the guitar.

"Someone, I have no idea who he was, picked me up and gave me a ride. We started talking about why I had dirt all over me and what was in the bag. I carried the bag in my upturned palms as if it were a priceless jewel-encrusted egg. I told him that I had been to visit Blues Mullins. 'The greatest blues guitar player who ever lived. He had magic in his finger bones,' I said. I used to tell everyone that.

"As for what was in the bag, without thinking, I just said 'blues bones.' Next thing I know, it was in newspapers and music magazines. Everybody was talking about me and calling me 'Bones.' The story and nickname were good for publicity, so I tied the bag to my guitar neck and let it happen."

"So you didn't do some kind of voodoo spell and sell your soul?" I asked.

"I just let the people talk. I didn't see that it was hurting anything. Plus, it got Ole Joe some recognition. For a while, they even had to guard his grave. Guitar players came from everywhere to get some dirt from it. When I started writing children's music, I dropped the name Bones and removed the bag from my guitar. Didn't think it would sit too well with the parents. A lot of them knew about my nickname, but they were cool with it."

Cory turned another page in the album. "I guess if anything, I bought my soul back. A lot of people sell their souls and don't even know it. You don't have to have no magic spell to do it either. You just let greed or pride or an addiction take you over. Then you'll do anything to get what you want. Some folks lie and cheat their friends. Some steal and some even murder. Most never reclaim their soul, and it does them in. Look at all the great musicians who have lost their lives or careers to drugs or booze. I doubt any of them ever stepped foot in a graveyard at midnight. With or without a spell."

His words stopped. He sat staring at a picture of a short old black man with a beat-up guitar. The man in the photo was making a sad puppy-dog face that made him look like he was begging while he pointed to a whiskey bottle he held upside down in his other hand. "Joe sold his soul for the bottle. Never got it back."

The room got quiet. Like pure silence as if someone pressed the mute button for the room. Cory rubbed his fingers over Ole Joe's picture.

"So you don't know how to break the spell we did?" I asked.

"Don't know nothing about breaking hoodoo spells."

"Do you think things are going to keep getting worse?"

He flipped through a few more pages of the album. "Well, I don't know. But whether it's practice, magic, or God-given talent, you're playing a lot better now than when I first met you. Everybody's going to get hurt from time to time, and bad luck can haunt a body for what seems like forever. Sometimes if you believe in something strong enough, it can feel like magic or good luck.

If you believe you play better because you have a bag of bones, a rabbit's foot, or a pink and purple sock hanging from your guitar neck, you'll feel lost without it. When I first met you, you were scared to play in front of people. You worried about messing up. When you're here, who are you playing for? Who are you trying to impress?"

I'd never really thought about it before, but since Dad left, I didn't have to play *for* anybody. "Nobody. I'm just playing because it's fun."

"So, you're playing for yourself, right?"

"Yeah, I guess."

"That's why we musicians play music. At least that's why *I* play. For me. But I found that other people like to hear it, too." Cory's face lit up.

A low rumble of thunder made the glass in the live room rattle.

"When you're on stage," Cory continued, "play for yourself. Play your best and don't worry about the others who just might happen to hear. Your music comes from within you. That's where the real magic is. It's part of you. Just let it happen."

The thunder rumbled again.

"Can I use your phone to find a ride?" I asked. If it hadn't been storming, I would have walked. Anything was better than calling Jeff.

"Want me to give you a lift?"

"Wow, that would be great. Are you sure you don't mind?"

"No, it's fine." He closed the album and put it back in the file cabinet.

Now what? He hadn't done any kind of spell on the bag.

But we *had*.

chapter
TWENTY-THREE

THE RAIN STOPPED JUST BEFORE WE GOT TO MY house. Cory didn't want to come in, so he dropped me off and left. Jeff's police car was in the driveway and lights were on inside the house.

"Mom?" I shouted as I ran through the door.

"In here," Jeff called from her room.

"You okay?" I walked over and sat on the edge of the bed beside her. She looked pale and barely turned her head toward me. Jeff was arranging a pot of flowers with "get well soon" helium balloons floating above it on her dresser.

"I'm okay. How are you?" she said weakly and put her hand on mine. "Have you been in my bubble bath again?"

I guess the plastic zipper bag had popped open. I rolled up the grocery bag and walked toward the door. "No, I guess the smell didn't come out of these jeans from when I spilled it on them the other day," I lied. "I've got to change and call Max. Holler if you need anything."

"You and your Max," Mom said. "I'm fine. Just a little drugged from the pain pills."

I called Max to apologize for the way I had treated him at school. He said he thought the voodoo spells were turning me into something like Gollum. The way the ring did in *The Hobbit*. Then I told him how I chickened out from telling Cory about us taking his voodoo bag and how I put the real one back.

In bed, I stared at the poster and thought of what Cory had said about selling your soul by stealing and stuff. We had already stolen. I wondered if by returning the voodoo bag I had bought my soul back. I fell asleep thinking about Ole Joe Mullins.

Wednesday, at school, I was invisible. Myra barely

acknowledged that I existed. When I walked through the halls, no one so much as glanced at me. No air guitar. No "Rock on!" No nothing. Maybe returning Cory's bag had worked.

chapter TWENTY-FOUR

I KNEW THINGS WERE BACK TO NORMAL SATURDAY morning. Even the Internet had ignored me. The "Unplugged" count had stayed at 9,665 for the past three days.

Max and I arrived early to the talent show, and there were already hundreds of people in the seats. "Max, this isn't going to work."

"What's not going to work?" he asked.

"I think I'm going to hurl."

"Is that your stomach gurgling?" he said. "You're going to erupt."

"You've got to get Cory's voodoo bag. I can't do this without it."

"What, I just go to Cory's, break in, and take it —again?"

"Tell him I broke my backing track CD and need him to burn another one. While he's doing it, go upstairs and swap bags again." I handed him the fake bag. "And hurry!"

I figured it would take at least an hour for him to ride there and back. He would have plenty of time. It was 9:00, and the show was scheduled to start at 10:00. I was contestant ninety-eight.

"Welcome..."

All it took was hearing that one word over the P.A. system. I barely made it to the restroom.

Dry heaves suck.

At least I could sit down in the stall, and I had a place to hang my gig bag. At 10:48, I decided to go out and find Max. Without a word, he gave me the bag. I shoved it into my pocket, and he vanished into the crowd. I felt like we were in a spy movie.

At 11:00, I went to the Green Room. There were about a dozen guitar players in there. Lamon was being all smiley. I guess it was his job to try to make everyone feel like they could win. Mr. Encouragement. I wanted to throw up all over his clipboard.

"How's the finger, Rodney?" A voice came from behind me as I pulled my guitar from the gig bag.

When I spun around, I almost hit Eddie's nose with the end of it.

"You know, if you'd keep your nose out of other people's business, it might not be sore all the time." I really wished my guitar had hit him.

"You must be real good to play with that brace on. Oh yeah, I forgot. Your guitar plays itself." He grabbed the guitar. "Let's have a look."

He pulled the guitar from me and slapped my right hand away. Pain shot up my arm. I guess that's what set me off. I grabbed the guitar neck with my left hand and pulled. It was no use. He was stronger. The guitar slipped from my hand.

"Calm down, Rodney. I just want to take a look."

"Give it back. Now!" I grabbed it again, but my grasp was too weak. He pulled it from me then held the guitar in front of him, jabbing the neck toward me like it was some kind of medieval sword. I'm sure we looked like a couple of idiots doing a tribal dance, hopping back and forth from one foot to another in perfect timing.

He lunged toward me. I sidestepped and grabbed the guitar neck, but couldn't pull it from him.

"Boys!" Lamon yelled. Then he started talking

to someone on the headset microphone he was wearing.

The other kids backed up against the walls around the room.

Eddie turned his head to look at Lamon. Since I couldn't pull the guitar from his grip, I shoved it toward him.

If he hadn't been trying to use it like some kind of weapon, the body wouldn't have been in front of his head. If he hadn't turned his head to the left when Lamon yelled at us, Eddie's nose would have been where his right ear was when the guitar hit him there.

"Okay, boys, that's enough," a giant of a security guard said. "Come with me."

We followed him to an office in the back of the theater. Inside, he knocked on an adjoining door. A few seconds later, a tall thin man with a white beard walked in. He was wearing a white suit and black boots. He could have been Santa if he gained some weight. "Hello, boys. I'm Walter Crocket. Welcome to my theater. What's the problem here today?"

Eddie started to speak, but I blurted out, "He grabbed my—"

"One at a time," Mr. Crocket said. "Whose guitar is that?"

"It's mine," I said. "He took it."

"What's your name"—he looked at the tag hanging around my neck—"number zero-nine-eight?"

"I'm Rodney Becker."

"Is this true? Did you take his guitar"—he looked at Eddie's tag—"number zero-nine-nine? And who are you?"

"I'm Eddie Manford." He looked stupid holding his ear with his elbow stuck straight out. "You've probably heard of my dad. I just wanted to look at it. He has something wired up inside it that plays through the amplifier when he flips the pickup selector or something. He should be disqualified for cheating. He can't play with that thing on his finger."

Mr. Crocket looked at me. One corner of his mouth twisted up. "Well, let's find out." He nodded at the security guard. "Johnny, call one of the guitar techs and tell him to bring his tool kit." He took the guitar from the security guard and started pulling off the knobs. A moment later, some guy walked in with a small briefcase.

"Seems the boy might be having a problem with his guitar," Mr. Crocket said. "Can you check it out? Might have something to do with the wiring inside."

The guy opened his briefcase. It was full of tools and test meters, each sticking in its own special pocket.

"Sure thing," the technician said. He took out an orange and black cordless drill fitted with a peg winder attachment and loosened each string. Then he pulled off the tip of the pickup selector, took out a small screwdriver, and removed the screws from the pickguard. We all gathered closer as he lifted the plastic piece from the guitar.

"Don't you need a search warrant for something like this?" I asked.

I wanted to hit Eddie in the nose again for starting everything, and I wanted to punch Max for talking me into letting him rig up the MP3 player.

"No," Mr. Crocket said. "The papers your parents signed give us permission to examine any and all personal property brought into the theater. It's in the fine print." He nodded, scrunched his nose, and made finger quotes in the air. "You know, 'Homeland Security' and all."

"Everything looks good here," the technician said. "Wait a minute." He pulled out a small flashlight from his case. "It's been modified. Looks like some extra wires coming from the back."

The technician turned the mess of a guitar over and removed the back cover. After tugging at the duct tape, he held up a circuit board with a small display screen. "Looks like someone pulled the cover off an MP3 player and wired it in." He pointed the beam from the light back into the guitar. "And the tremolo system has a blue dog's bone stuck in it." Everyone looked at me with puzzled expressions.

"Told ya." Eddie was still holding his ear. "He should be disqualified for cheating." He gave me one of his stupid grins.

My hand found its way to the bulge of the voodoo bag in my pocket. I stepped toward Mr. Crocket. "I never used it! I don't need it." I pointed back toward Eddie. "He should be disqualified for taking my guitar and starting a fight."

"That's enough," Mr. Crocket said. "Calm down, young man." He looked at Eddie. "The auditions are over, and it's just your word against his. Technically, he hasn't done anything wrong today. He hasn't cheated since he hasn't performed yet." He looked from Eddie to me. "If Mr. Zero-

Nine-Eight can perform using another guitar, which I will provide, he's still in."

"Sure," I said, "I can do that." I returned Eddie's stupid grin. "Do you have a Strat I can use?"

chapter
TWENTY-FIVE

"Last call for contestant number zero-nine-eight," a voice boomed throughout the theater.

I patted the bag in my pocket and ran to center stage. There were about a million people looking at me. I'm sure I looked like a dork standing there holding the end of the guitar cord looking for somewhere to plug it in.

"Would you please approach the microphone and tell everyone your name?" The voice boomed again over the loudspeakers.

"I'm Rodney Becker," I announced. Some guy walked on stage and took the end of my guitar cord.

"And what will you be playing for us today?"

"My blues song."

I noticed Max sitting in the third row with his mom's video camera. "It's called the 'Bow Wow Blues.'" Max smiled and gave me a thumbs-up.

Chuckles swept through the audience. I felt my face heating up. I wiped the sweat from my hands onto my pants. When my track started to play, the house lights went down.

Pain shot up my right hand and into my arm when I gripped my guitar pick. My fingers trembled, and I bumped the brace on the high E string. I made it through the first three seconds and stopped. "We get five minutes to perform, right?" I spoke to the spotlight that was blinding me. My backing track stopped. "Can you start my track over? And can you turn all the lights off 'til the intro is finished?"

A slow monotone voice answered over the P.A. system, "Sure, Mr. Becker, you're the star."

I pulled the brace from my finger and let it drop to the floor. The room filled with a low rumble. Everyone probably thought I had lost it. I thought about sneaking off stage when they turned off the lights. Eyes closed, I waited.

I imagined being in my room playing with the lights out and those twenty thousand eyes staring at me from my poster.

My click track started.

Click.

I thought about the rabbit's foot the guy had worn on his guitar strap.

Click.

I thought about Ole Joe's guitar pick inside the voodoo bag in my pocket.

Click.

I thought about how Dad hated my music.

Click.

Heat poured across my face, but not from inside me. Through my closed eyelids, I could sense the brightness of the spotlight.

I played the first eight notes of my song. Cory was right. It sounded like the CD, but it was way louder. Concert loud. I must have zoned out, because while I played, I couldn't feel the pain in my finger. Those three minutes went by like seconds.

The place exploded with applause. I had done it. I had played for me and let everyone else listen. The house lights came on, and I saw Max, Cory, Mom, and Jeff three rows from the front. I never knew that with all the lights off, and with a spotlight shining down on you, you couldn't see all the eyeballs looking back.

I couldn't move. I closed my eyes, tilted my head back, and listened. And laughed.

Was this what Dad was chasing? What he was willing to give up everything for? Including Mom and me? Maybe Mom was right.

Maybe I am like him.

I want it, too.

"It's over, Rodney. You can leave the stage now." The announcer's lifeless voice broke my trance.

I bowed to the audience as I unplugged the guitar cord and let it fall to the floor. I then blew them a kiss, shook my guitar over my head, and ran off stage.

"Where's Myra?" I asked Cory when I made it to where they were.

"Over there." Cory pointed to the first row. She was sitting with some other girls from school. It looked like they were having a great time from the way they were laughing.

Eddie started to play, but without a backing track. He didn't need one because he sounded awesome as always.

After Eddie had played this cool intro, every kid

in the place started singing: *"It's going to be another happy day. I can tell by the way the sun is shining."*

"What the—?" Cory shouted above the music.

It was "Another Happy Day" from one of Cory's TV shows.

All the parents joined in.

"I'm flattered," Cory said. "I wondered whatever happened to that piece of sheet music I was transcribing for Myra. She told me she lost it."

I guess Eddie had found it but hadn't known it was a kid's song. When he realized what was happening, he stopped playing, unplugged his guitar, and ran off stage.

The crowd kept singing: "The clouds are happy too, floating in the sky of blue so high."

"Rodney," came a voice from behind me. I felt a hand on my shoulder.

I spun around. "Dad?" Maybe the spell was working.

"You'll have to teach me some of those licks."

"It wasn't country. What are you doing here?" I asked.

"We came to see you," he said.

I didn't know what to say. Or do. I felt like I was choking on something and had to swallow real hard to make my throat work. "Thanks," was all I could get out. I swallowed again and cleared my throat.

"Yeah, dude." Jimmy, his bass player, said. "Plus your mom said he had to get the rest of his junk out of your house or she was tossing it."

"Oh yeah," Dad said. "When this is over, I have something out in the car for you. Don't let me forget."

Everyone went quiet when a string section started to play. It was her. The redheaded girl from the audition. She had an electric guitar strapped on, but she was playing a classical guitar mounted on some kind of microphone stand. She played fingerstyle through the intro, then hit an open chord and let the guitar ring while she stepped back, grabbed the pick from her mouth, and began to play the electric guitar. The backing track went into some kind of heavy metal sounding orchestration, and she kicked into what sounded like a cross between Jimmy Page and Eddie Van Halen. I wasn't the only one who thought she was awesome. The crowd went crazy and shot to their feet for a standing ovation.

When Dad opened the car trunk I thought I would pass out. It was my guitar. "Wow. Are you sure?"

He opened the case. "Yeah, oh nines are too light. And here's your strap. That thing's dangerous. It could ruin a guitar."

He handed me my worn out strap and the new pack of strings I had bought before he took the guitar. He smiled and closed the case.

"Oh, I forgot you use heavier gauge strings." I guess I was crazy for thinking he was bringing my guitar back to me. Guess the voodoo spell wasn't that strong after all.

"Want to have lunch tomorrow before we have to head out?"

"Doesn't matter." I knew he would find something more important to do.

"It's a date," he said.

chapter
TWENTY-SIX

DAD SURPRISED ME AND PICKED ME UP ON SUNDAY like he'd said he would. We ate lunch at the Old Mill, where he told me all about his band's new job playing seven nights a week in Nashville. It had been a long time since we just talked. I had forgotten how excited he got when he talked about playing music. All I wanted to talk about was how I felt onstage, but it was all about him. As always.

"So, how is it that you're here?" I asked when we ordered dessert. "Why didn't you have to play last night?"

"I told the boss I had to attend a very important music event yesterday, and I needed a couple days off. We've got to be back tomorrow. I'm pretty sure she thinks we went somewhere to audition. Maybe she'll raise our pay to keep us." Dad stabbed a huge berry with his fork from his strawberry shortcake and raised it in the air like a victory salute.

I thought about asking why he took back my guitar, but for the first time in a long time, we weren't arguing. Besides, since I had stuck Einstein's bone in my old guitar, I actually liked *it* better.

I wondered if the real reason he came to the show was for me. Or because Mom told him he had to get his stuff and to come to the show since he was in town anyway. Or if it was the voodoo. I wasn't sure I really wanted to know.

When I got home, Mom handed me a message to call Victoria Valentine. "Isn't she that cute redhead who won in your age group yesterday? You think she wants to rub it in that you let a girl beat you?" Mom tilted her head and gave me one of her crooked smiles.

"She beat a *lot* of guys, not just me." I took the note to my room and dialed her number.

"Hello?"

"Victoria? This is Rodney Becker. My mom said you called."

"Yeah. I wanted to catch you after the awards yesterday, but you were gone before I could get off the stage. I caught up with Myra and got your number."

"Yeah, all those photos and awards. I guess it's a tough life, being a winner and all," I said and laughed. At first there was silence, and then she started laughing, too.

"I was wondering if you play in a band."

"No. I don't know if I'm good enough."

"Well, that's what practice is for. You were good enough to get fifth place yesterday."

So were four others, I thought. Except they were better—a lot better.

"Here's the deal. The Volunteer Band Battles are going to be held at Patriot Park in Pigeon Forge this July. I need a guitar player because everything has to be live. No recorded tracks. First practice is tomorrow night at seven. My place."

"Why are you calling a fifth-place loser to join your band?"

"You were the next one on my list."

There was silence. I wasn't her first choice? I wondered why the others had turned her down.

"You still there?" she asked. "I'm joking. Did you see those other guys? They were just playing to impress. I need someone who wants to play for real."

"You were pretty impressive," I said.

"Thanks. I was impressed by your playing, too. Not the *way* you played, though. You looked like you were off in another world somewhere. The judges consider stage presence, too. Which you don't have. We'll have to work on that. It may be why you didn't win. So, do you want to join the band? You don't have to audition since I've heard you play."

I couldn't believe she had called me, much less asked me to join her band. "I guess. If you think I'm good enough."

"Sure, I want only the best. I do most of the lead vocals, but you'll get to do a few and sing backup on the others."

"That might be a problem," I said. "I don't sing."

"What do you mean? You lip-sync?"

"No, I've never tried." I held up the voodoo bag by its drawstring and watched it twirl. "I'll see what I can find in my little bag of tricks, though."

"That's what practice is for. We'll work on the singing. Give me your email address, and I'll send directions."

I gave her the address and told her I would have to talk to Mom and email her back.

I had tons of emails waiting to congratulate me on my performance at the competition. Max also congratulated me for beating Eddie. I graciously accepted the victory. After all, it wasn't my fault he was disqualified for leaving the stage.

In another email, Max had included a link to what he said was a hot new video. It was of Eddie at the competition. It started with a close-up of him when he realized that all the kids were singing. Then it panned to show them. It looked like a concert for preschoolers. The hit count was already at six hundred, and it had a ton of comments about him playing children's songs. One person asked him if he wanted to join The Big Bird Band.

When I checked my video, the view count hadn't changed. I guess everyone got tired of watching me do nothing.

Victoria had sent an attachment with a full color map showing how to get to her house. I replied, telling her that I would be there. I also forwarded the link Max had sent so she could watch Eddie's video.

I was so excited about going to Victoria's the next evening that I couldn't sleep. At 12:04, I got up and played around with my guitar. I decided to tie the voodoo bag to the neck to see how it would look. I knew I would eventually have to return it to Cory and thought I could make one of my own. That would have to be easier than lopping off a rabbit's foot. I guess we had been a little rough with Cory's bag because some of the stitches had come loose on top. When I pulled a string, the rest of them fell out.

I removed the small box from inside. It was an old matchbox. All the writing had faded off the top, but there was a place on its side to strike a match. I slid the box open as far as it would go, which was just a little over halfway. It felt like something inside was holding it. I turned it over and dumped everything out. There was a silver ring. I figured it was the one that had belonged to Cory's grandmother. It looked like it had been worn a lot because it was thin in a couple of places.

There were also the dice Cory had told me about. The corners had been rounded off, and when I rolled them, they took forever to stop. It was like rolling marbles with numbers on them. It was creepy knowing they were made from somebody's bones.

Ole Joe's guitar pick was thin and brittle. It was

cracked and felt like it would crumble at the slightest touch. The small hole in it made me wonder if Cory might have worn it as a necklace at one time.

As I was putting everything back into the box, I noticed something stuck on the inside. I grabbed an ink pen to pry it loose. It made a hollow, tinny sound when it fell on my wooden desktop. At first, I wasn't sure what it was. It took about a minute for me to figure out where I had seen something like it before. It must have turned dark with age. The model that Dr. Sanders had shown me at the clinic was solid white. I held it up to the tip of my index finger and imagined it being inside my skin like the one on my X-ray. Then I really got creeped out. I guess my mind was playing tricks on me because I swore I heard someone whisper, "Gimme dat."

NOTE FROM THE AUTHOR

If you enjoyed the book, please consider leaving a review, and look for book two, *At the Crossroads*, coming soon! To stay up-to-date on all of Rick Starkey's books, visit his website https:// RickStarkey.com or subscribe to his newsletter http://eepurl.com/bv-FNz.

Blues Bones was originally published by publisher Leap Books LLC. Leap Books closed April 26, 2019. We were in the final stages of edits of At The Crossroads, Blues Bones Book Two when this happened, and all rights of book one and book two reverted to me. I decided to self publish and contacted Kelly Hashway, the editor for Leap Books who acquired the original Blues Bones but left Leap Books not long after book one was released. Hashway, a professional freelance editor and USA Today bestselling author, was a lifesaver. To the best editor ever, thank you! (KellyHashway.com)

ACKNOWLEDGMENTS

I would like to send a special thanks to the following people for helping make this book possible:

To Kelly Hashway, the best editor an author could ever have, for falling in love with this book the first time you read it. And for your guidance and answers to my endless questions, (even the crazy ones like how to put a smiley in a text message :).)

To Shannon Delany and everyone at Leap Books for believing in this project.

To copy editor, Trisha Wooldridge, for seeing the things I didn't. And to Nina Gautier Gee and Shannon Delany, for the original.

To my wife, Betty, for the time and encouragement to keep writing. And for all those mouse clicks that sent me away to writer's conferences and workshops.

To my mom, Mildred Starkey, for all the guitars and amplifiers you and Dad bought me.

To my sister, Ann Bentley, for always believing I could do this. And for all the spooky tales and times we've had through the years. We both know we heard the doll sing.

To my kids, Sonya, Trina, and Tylor, and the rest of my family for understanding how much time writing takes and how much time it takes away.

To Jan Fields, for all the questions you answer on the Writers Retreat.

To Katie Clark and Gail Kamer, for your honest critiques and input on the early drafts.

To Gennifer Choldenko, Deborah Halverson, April Lurie, and Nancy Butts for sharing your time and knowledge with me.

To Mandy, for the idea of what to fix Rodney's guitar with so it would stay in tune. For our early morning writing sessions and playing "gimmie dat."

To Joel and Jim at the Music Outlet, thank you for all the guitars, gear, and technical information through the years.

To Robert Prophit, for spreading the word about Rodney Becker.

ALSO BY RICK STARKEY

At The Crossroads

Blues Bones Book Two

Beyond Midnight

Blues Bones Book Three

(coming soon)

ABOUT THE AUTHOR

Rick Starkey is a graduate of the Institute of Children's Literature. He lives in a 200-year-old log cabin in the Great Smoky Arts and Crafts Community in Gatlinburg, Tennessee, where he and his wife, Betty, own and run Make It Magic, a magic shop and craft store. A day in Rick's life includes recommending and performing magic tricks for customers of all ages, carving bears from logs with a chainsaw, playing his guitar, and working on his next novel.

facebook.com/RickStarkeyWrites

twitter.com/RJStarkey

instagram.com/rickjstarkey

Made in the USA
Lexington, KY
21 November 2019